The Strip Mall Series: Book 1

BANANAS & DONUTS

t. torrest

CHAPTER 1

Three o'clock in the morning.

That's what time I woke up for work every single day. I took my shower, got dressed, and threw my hair in its usual ponytail. And then I drove—in the dark, mind you—to get to the bakery by four.

Every. Single. Day.

I knew going into this gig that the hours were pretty brutal. But the fact of the matter is, I wouldn't have had it any other way. I love my job.

My name is Stefanie ~~Manzo~~ Keefe and I'm the owner and self-proprietor of *Smoochycakes*, the best damned bakery in the entire state of Pennsylvania. Specialty cakes, kickass cookies, melt-in-your-mouth pastries... and our "Delectable Donuts" are to die for. They were my own personal creation and the main thing that put us on the map.

I always knew I wanted to be a baker. I did it my entire life just for fun, but by the time I graduated college, decided to finally get serious about it.

I'd kicked off my training at two New York City institutions: *Le Pain Quotidien* on Bleecker to learn the basics, then *Butter Lane* on 7th to round out my flavoring education. Another two years spent at various culinary institutes in order to learn every cake technique on the planet, plus an added year at the

School of Visual Arts to hone some sculpting skills. Then I worked as an apprentice for almost three years, realizing soon after that it was time to open my own place. Eventually, I managed to land a spot in the much-coveted *Rimmer Strip Mall.*

Yeah, yeah, I can hear you snickering. Those of us that live in such a dubiously-named town have heard all the jokes before. Fact is, Rimmer happens to be pretty awesome, stupid name and all. Besides, I could never decide who was worse: The numbskulls who named this town... or me, for choosing to live in it.

I'm originally from New Jersey, the Mall Capital of the World. So what was I thinking when I decided to open a bakery in Pennsylvania?

If you've ever encountered my cheating scumbag of an ex-husband, you'd know the answer to that. And if you ever encountered him, there's a good chance you may have even slept with him. That's not a reflection on you, by the way. I just figure that if he managed to stick his dick into as many women as I suspect he did, then a case could be made regarding the law of averages.

The case *I* made, however, was divorce on the grounds of "Irretrievable Breakdown," which could also conveniently describe my mental state at that time. I packed up my stuff and drove my piece of shit car straight down Route 80. I had no destination in mind, but the opposite coast was looking pretty appealing right about then. Only ninety minutes into my getaway, however, my car broke down, and that's how I was introduced to the town of Rimmer. Quaint, charming, an entire state away... I figured it was as good a place as any to start a new life.

That was almost two years ago. I've been here ever since.

I pulled my Jeep Cherokee into my usual spot in the back lot and grabbed the box of T-shirts from the cargo hold to bring inside. I'd just ordered some new tees to celebrate the launch of our bacon-infused line of sweet treats.

Yeah, okay, I know that sounds weird. But bacon seems to be all the rage these days, and believe it or not, a candied-bacon donut actually tastes pretty damn good.

Just as I slammed the hatch, my next-store-neighbor appeared in his open doorway.

Ugh. Couldn't I have one day that didn't start with Jesse Dickface Miller?

If I'm going to be honest, I'll admit that okay, fine, Jesse was hardly a dickface. Dark, messy hair that always looked like he just rolled out of bed. Mischievous topaz eyes. A body that could rival Michelangelo's David, save for the micropeen. Presumably.

Not that I cared. His good looks were the *second* most outstanding thing about him. The first being his unrelenting arrogance.

Fact is, Jesse was the King of Smarm, put on this earth to do nothing more than fuck random women and annoy the living shit out of me. I don't think I've ever had one conversation with the guy that didn't end in an argument, which is a shame, because he was actually pretty funny.

And smart. And hot.

If I could just have one day when he wasn't so intent on shocking me in some way, I could almost envision a scenario where we could be friends.

That day was not today.

Jesse wrapped his fingers around his coffee mug as he leaned against the door frame. "Mornin', Sugar Tits."

See what I mean?

It was simply easier to remain civil. *Do not engage.* I braced a knee against the door to balance the box on my thigh while I fiddled with my keys. "Morning, Jesse."

"Can I help you out with your box?"

His raised eyebrow didn't escape my notice, but there was no way I was going to acknowledge his leading comment. "Thanks, but I can handle it."

"I do love to watch a woman take care of her own box..."

I would have laughed, but that would only encourage him. So instead, I shot back, "Probably because you're too selfish to take care of it for her?"

"Hey, I offered to do it, didn't I?" He took a sip from his coffee mug before adding, "One of these days, I'm hoping you'll let me."

The guy had been hitting on me for the better part of an entire year. I didn't take it personally; that's just who he was. He was on a constant quest to get laid, which made him no better than my man-whore ex-husband. He was lucky that we didn't work together. I'd have sued him for sexual harassment ten times over by now.

Jesse ran *The Market* next door, so he and I were normally the first ones here—I always needed to get the ovens cranking, and he needed to accept his produce deliveries—and it seemed he couldn't go a single morning without trying to antagonize me in some way. And the more worked up I got, the more amused he became. Half-asleep and pissed-off was no way to start a day.

I let the door slam behind me as I flipped on the lights with my elbow and welcomed the scent of my kitchen, that uniquely sweet aroma that always boosted my mood. The smell of buttercream danced on every inhale; it was embedded in the floorboards and in every crevice. I could almost taste it as I effected a deep yawn and deposited the box on one of the counters.

Needless to say, the first thing I did was to make the coffee.

While it was brewing, I went about my morning ritual, pre-heating the ovens and setting out the day's ingredients. I hadn't been doing much actual baking over the past months—managing the nitty gritty of this place took up most of my time—but due to circumstances beyond my control, I recently found myself back in the kitchen yet again.

When Smoochycakes first opened sixteen months ago, I was afraid to entrust the baking to anyone other than Yours Truly. After the place was up and running, however, I realized I would burn out pretty quickly if I didn't delegate some of my workload.

I hired a phenomenal head baker fresh out of culinary school, and shifted my focus toward maintaining the business end of things. Things were going pretty well... until I was forced to fire her only one month into her reign.

I hired a sweet, albeit subpar replacement out of pure desperation, but that little move sure did a number on my bottom line. Business hasn't exactly been booming. I was actually grateful when she told me she was quitting to move to Wyoming with her boyfriend. That circumstance required me to assume my old position as head baker until I could find a new one. After only two weeks playing both roles, however, I could already feel the stress piling up. I needed to find a new head baker—and fast.

I fixed myself a mug of coffee and settled into my "office," a postage-stamp-sized corner of the storeroom where I was able to cram a desk between two metal bookshelves that held all our dry goods. I tackled some paperwork before checking the list of the day's orders... and crap. Right there on the top of the pile was Mrs. Feinstein's invoice for four strawberry shortcakes.

Shit. Jesse was supposed to order strawberries for me. Which meant that I now had to deal with him in order to pick them up.

I grumbled as I pushed away from my desk and went outside to the back lot again. The Market's door was still opened, so I gave a quick knock before heading inside.

And what to my wondering eyes should appear but a half-dressed Jesse Miller in all his beautiful glory.

Whoa.

CHAPTER 2

I froze in my tracks, stunned by the sight of his naked torso. His back was turned, allowing me a moment to appreciate his bulging biceps. His strong shoulders tapered into a trim waist, accentuating the faded jeans that were slung low on his slim hips, exposing two perfect dimples above his luscious ass. The guy may have been a world-class antagonist but I couldn't deny that he was fabulous-looking.

He turned toward me, and I was able to catch a glimpse of his smooth, hard chest before his voice jogged me out of my gaping. "Ever hear of knocking?"

I shook myself out of the stupor to shoot back, "I did. Ever hear of health codes? Why are you hanging out in your stockroom half-naked?"

He grabbed a kelly-green tee off a shelf and pulled it over his head. I tried not to notice the delectable view as he tugged the shirt down over his rock-hard abs. "Not hanging out. You simply caught me as I was changing my shirt." He gripped his hands around the edge of the steel counter behind him and leaned back, his lip twitching as he added, "You lucky girl, you."

The overabundance of testosterone was too much for me to handle. I was still recuperating from the sight of his incredible body, and now he was shooting that damnable smirk in my direction? As much as I tried to deny it, I couldn't help my body's response to such oozing male sex appeal, and I found myself mentally chastising my throbbing lady bits.

"Wrong. I just always have bad timing."

Thing was, my bad timing had more to do with my philandering ex than anything that was happening here between Jesse and me. But even though he could hardly be blamed for my failed marriage, there was more bite to my statement than intended.

Jesse noticed.

His head cocked to the side as his eyes tightened. "I thought you were done being The Queefmonster."

Ha! When your last name is Keefe, queef isn't too far a stretch. Trust me. I endured four entire years of high school with that nickname. But queefmonster was a new one, and, I had to admit, a pretty good one as well. "The *what?*"

"Don't get your panties in a twist. I meant it as a compliment."

"I'll ask you kindly to leave my panties out of this conversation." My lip twitched against my will as I added, "And for the record, *queefmonster* hardly sounds like a compliment."

"It wasn't. The fact that you *haven't been* The Queefmonster was the compliment. You've been an almost normal person the past couple of weeks."

The guy was observant, I had to give him that.

The thing was, I never used to give Jesse an inch. When I first met him, I thought he was pretty entertaining. His flirty comments were intriguing, not annoying. If I hadn't been so caught up in my own bullshit, maybe I could have appreciated that more. But I was too broken at that point in my life to indulge in his game. I was angry about my failed marriage and stressed about getting my new business off the ground.

Jesse was relentless, however. He was determined to loosen me up, and with his offbeat sense of humor, it was hard to keep my walls in place. I started to think it wouldn't be the worst thing in the world if the two of us could maybe learn to be friends.

And then, mere days later, he had to go and ruin it.

Any friendship we'd been working toward had been destroyed before it even had a chance to begin.

But recently—ever since I started baking again—I guess my spirits had been raised. Being back in my kitchen made me happy, even when dealing with Jesse. The past couple of weeks, he and I had actually been getting along better than we ever had. And it's really been kinda great.

Until now.

His little psychoanalysis was still echoing in the air between us as the memory of his betrayal played across my mind, firing me up all over again. My voice turned sour as I snipped, "Thanks, but I'm not looking for a personality assessment. I only came here to get my strawberries."

He crossed his arms over his chest and stared me down. "Why do you hate me so much?"

His toffee eyes bored into mine, causing an involuntary shiver to race along my spine. Not that I'd ever let him know it. "Isn't it obvious?"

"Obviously not."

"Okay fine," I started in. "You want reasons? How about this: You're a slut. You're infuriating. You're belligerent, cocky, arrogant—"

"What you call arrogance, others would call charming."

Interesting that he didn't feel the need to defend the other adjectives I'd used to describe him. "Wasn't so 'charming' when you targeted my best baker."

"Sure it was."

"I had to fire her because of you!"

"Who says?"

My head almost exploded. Was he really that dense? "Ummm... society? You fucked her behind my display counter!"

The bastard actually had the gall to smile. "So?"

"*So? SO?* Your little rendezvous took place during business hours! I had to close down for the rest of the day while I disinfected the store. Thank God the Health Department didn't catch wind of it. I could have lost my entire business!"

"Oh, come on," he said, leveling a brow at me. "Are you really still holding a grudge about something that happened over a year ago?"

"Yes!"

"Besides," he went on, "it's not like we put on a show. It was a slow day. There were no customers in there."

"There could have been!"

"But there weren't."

"But there could have been."

"Not with the way you run that place."

My hands went involuntarily to my hips. "I beg your pardon?"

He let out with a calming breath, switching gears. "C'mon, Stef. Within the first month of you opening your doors, the place was swarming with customers. You were on your way. I mean, the whole reason you started this business was because you loved to bake, right?"

"Yeah, so?"

"Well, only a few short months later, you abandoned your kitchen. Your customers have been dropping off like flies because of it. You jumped the shark when you started delegating everything to your staff."

As much as I didn't want to face it, he had a point. My bakery *had* done really well in the beginning, and yeah, duh, I was the one doing all the baking back then. As much as I loved it, there were so many other tasks that needed my attention, and soon enough, *running* the place became my full-time job. I'd gotten bogged down in the managerial role of my business, a duty I'd delusionally believed would come secondary to any actual baking. Huh.

It should have been obvious, but it took Jesse's blunt assertion for me to realize it was true. I didn't want to admit any of that to him, however. What I wanted was to kick him right in his perfect white teeth.

"You gonna just stand there staring at me or are you going to admit I'm right?"

He just stood there expectantly in an unbroken pose as I snapped back into form. Who cared what Jesse Miller thought about my life? Aside from hellos and goodbyes every day, he wasn't a part of my life at all!

The newfound resolve bolstered my stance as I sneered, "I'm not doing this today. Can't you find some poor unsuspecting tart to annoy?"

"Aww, now Stef. You know you're my favorite tart."

I was agitated and frustrated and pissed at him for forcing me to face my shortcomings. Nobody wants their weaknesses thrown in their face. "You need to go to hell, Jesse."

"You need to get laid, Stefanie."

My mouth dropped at his words. For all our off-color exchanges, he'd never before resorted to such a rude personal attack. I stood there, gawking at him, speechless and infuriated. He stared back, unflinching.

The energy crackled between us, tense and electrifying. His eyes darkened as he eyed me up and down, the look on his face feral and imposing. My heart started pounding a demanding staccato in my chest as we locked onto one another, neither one of us willing to break the heated standoff.

Before I knew what was happening, Jesse closed the gap between us in three long strides. Suddenly, his arms were around my waist and his lips were slamming down on mine.

What the hell?

If I were a stronger woman with even an ounce of remaining pride, I would have pushed him away. I *should* have pushed him away. I should have slapped him. But instead, my traitorous body reacted involuntarily against the onslaught, and my breath hitched as his full lips slanted fiercely across mine. The kiss was forceful, punishing... and totally fucking hot.

I couldn't stop it. I didn't *want* to stop it. Fact was, Jesse's firm length pressing against mine was doing crazy things to my insides, and I didn't ever want the feeling to end. I felt the tension drain from my body as my muscles relaxed and my eyes closed on their own, my brain going down in willing defeat.

I breathed in, catching the sweet, fruity scent of him, and as his lips parted, I realized he tasted just as delicious. His tongue swept inside to tangle with mine as his hands angled down my spine, across my ass, pulling me tighter against his hard-on. Jesus. Feeling his hard cock rubbing against my pelvis turned me on more than I cared to admit. I stood on my tiptoes and slid my hands into his hair, prouder than I should have been at the groan that wrenched from his throat. Then again, I was doing some involuntary moaning of my own.

I couldn't control the hammering of my heart. I couldn't keep my limbs from trembling. I couldn't stop myself from grinding against that *magnificent fucking cock.*

Once Jesse knew he'd won me over, he pulled back just enough to whisper, "So what do you say, Stef? Wanna fuck?"

Idiot.

His asinine comment was enough to break the spell. I pushed against his chest, separating his body from mine.

"What?" he snickered. "I thought I could help you out!"

My palms were itching to slap him, but I managed to keep my hands to myself as I turned on my heel and stomped off.

CHAPTER 3

I was at the wrapping station in the back room under the guise of "organizing," but really all I was doing was looking for an excuse to slam things around. I shoved boxes back on their proper shelves, stabbed scissors into the storage block, and smashed paper into the garbage with blind fury. All the while, Jesse's words were pinging around my brain: *"You need to get laid."*

Who *says* that? Who the hell did he think he was? Stupid, gorgeous, conceited fucker. Where did he get off?

As much as I tried to push the conversation from my mind, I couldn't stop thinking about what he said. I couldn't stop thinking about that *kiss*. I shook my head, ridding myself of the memory. The last thing I needed was to get all worked up. That's kind of why I found myself in this position to begin with.

I mean, maybe if Jesse wasn't such a proficient slut, he wouldn't have been able to get me to cave so easily. Then again, maybe if I hadn't kept my hoo-hoo under lock and key for so damn long, I would have found it easier to resist him. The last time I had sex had been a looong time ago. I started to calculate the actual chasm, but the math got too depressing too fast.

Shit. Jesse was right. I really needed to get laid.

The question was: Why would *he* be the guy to break my dry spell?

I mean, he *was* totally hot—well, I guess if you were into that whole washboard-abs kind of thing. Too bad those bumpy obliques were attached to an utter douchenozzle.

Although, if I was going to be honest, I'd have to admit that he wasn't a *complete* asshole. There were times when he and I would genuinely have actual human conversations. Even when he was being a cad, his daily teasing was more flirty than irritating. It's just that I was such an insecure wuss that I always allowed his comments to get to me.

Huh. Maybe *I* was the problem.

While I was stewing from Jesse's comment, the jerkasaurus in question poked his head around the corner. "Hey, Keefecake. You forgot your strawberries."

Despite my indignation, the new nickname almost had me busting out into a laughing fit. "Keefecake?"

He shrugged, offering casually, "If it makes you feel any better, I'll let you make fun of my name, too. Just a suggestion: Most chicks refer to me as Jesse Miller: Pussy Killer."

That damn grin of his sucked me in against my will, and I suddenly found it easy to return his joking banter. "More like Pussy *Chiller*. Because the thought of you anywhere near that thing makes my blood run cold."

"Let's just compromise and call me Pussy Filler. I'll let you use your imagination as to why."

"Are you trying to say you have a big dick? I mean you *are* one, but I don't think that's what you were going for."

"Hey, I'll have you know that my dick is a legend around here."

"Nope. Wrong again. Hate to break it to you, but everyone says you're a *legendary dick*. Not the same thing."

"You're the only one who says that."

His playful tone was gone, replaced by a look of hurt in his eyes. It was enough for me to call a truce. I'd already come to the conclusion that my perpetual negativity had at least partially contributed to the ongoing rift between us, and I wanted to make things right. "I don't think you're a dick, Jesse." I ran a hand through my hair, stalling while I mustered up the courage to offer an apology—not just for the bickering this morning, but for a year's worth of bad attitude. "And also... I'm sorry that I've been on the rag for an entire year."

Jesse accepted my apology with a silent nod of his head.

Good. I hoped this would be a new chapter for us, a place to start from scratch. I was just so tired of finding reasons to be angry with him.

The vibe between us was bordering on serious, and I smiled in order to lighten the mood. "After all, you *did* bring my strawberries."

The change of subject shook off the last of our awkwardness, and caused Jesse to perk back up. "You should try one." His lip quirked as he added, "You know, just to make sure they're good."

I had a feeling he was asking me to test drive something more than just a strawberry. That thought was confirmed as he plucked one from the box and held it toward my lips. It was a seemingly effortless skill of his, the way he always managed to steer our interactions toward sex. I hated to admit it, but I was learning to be okay with that. I could say it was because I was feeling all warm and squishy from our talk, but actually, I wanted him to see that I could play, too. Hell, he wasn't the only sexy beast in the room.

I leaned forward toward his outstretched hand and closed my lips around the forbidden fruit, looking right into his eyes as I took a bite. He couldn't seem to find a way to stop staring at my mouth, and I swear I heard a low rumble coming from the back of his throat.

"Mmm. Delicious."

His lids were lowered as his voice caught. "Can I have a taste?"

Before I could stop him, he stepped closer and ran the pad of his thumb along my lower lip. His delicate touch shot a tremble across my skin and caused my brain to short-circuit. His eyes met mine as he sucked the juice off his fingertip, never once breaking my gaze.

Despite my wishes to the contrary, my insides started throbbing at the look on his face, my heartbeat thrumming in a dangerous cadence. It was near-impossible to collect a breath into my lungs; I finally managed that monumental task only for it to be released in a choppy exhale.

"My offer was genuine, Stef. I can help you out. I can make you forget yourself for a little while." He brushed the strawberry along my bottom lip before dipping his head closer to my ear, scratching out in a lethal whisper, *"All you need to do is say yes."*

When he pulled back, I could see the question in his eyes. I licked my lips in answer, and that's all the invitation Jesse needed. Before I knew what was happening, his mouth was on mine. Again.

My heart was beating out of my chest as he brushed his lips against my own, the sweet, slow caress of his mouth causing long-forgotten tremors to race along my spine. His hand went around to the back of my neck, pulling me closer as his tongue made a leisurely slide against the seam of my lips, coaxing me to let him inside.

And when I did, the dam broke.

Our tongues tousled in pure madness as my hands knotted into his hair, devouring him with a passion I didn't even know I possessed. Jesse returned my hunger, sliding his hands underneath my ass and lifting me to sit on the counter before stepping between my thighs. I was already aching to feel him inside me as he shoved his hips against mine, pushing his impressive member insistently against the cradle of my thighs.

It wasn't enough.

I wiggled closer toward him, an attempt to relieve the ache building behind my jeans as I wrapped my legs around his waist. He pulled us even tighter together, his hardened cock writhing against me, our hot breath mingling, a groan escaping from my throat.

Holy fuck I'm dry-humping Jesse Miller.

He swiped my hair behind my ear and leaned in, his breath tickling my skin, his scratchy voice wooing me with his words. "We could be great together, Stef. I'll make it so good for you. No strings. Just sex. For as long as you want me."

I felt my brain liquefying, delirious from the images he was evoking. "You need this," he whispered, peppering my temple with soft kisses. He circled his hips against me *right in that perfect spot* and added, "*I* need this. I don't know how much longer I can wait to fuck you. Please don't make me wait anymore."

Just as I was about to lose myself, he pulled back, a wicked gleam in his eye. "Just a taste for now, Stef."

He slid his hands over my thighs, his thumbs meeting in the middle, applying a bit of pressure to the spot in between.

"Think about what I said. You know where to find me."

CHAPTER 4

As I was kneading some pie crust in the kitchen, the girls came in to start their day. They were a chatty bunch, even at the ungodly hour of six o'clock in the morning. I could hear them henning about in the storefront, stashing their purses under the counter, fixing themselves some coffee from the pot I put on for them ten minutes before.

I loved my crew. I was proud of the family I'd assembled to help me run this place. Three great girls who were smart, friendly, and loyal: Andrea was the workhorse, wide-eyed and optimistic, and willing to do any menial task that would help improve her craft. Kerry was bright and smiley, a true asset behind my front counter. And Helene was a combination of the both of them, with a little bit of me thrown in for good measure.

Normally, I'd find a few minutes to share a cuppa with my girls, go over the pickup orders, assign tasks for the day ahead. But that particular morning, I'd been hit with the bag of bricks otherwise known as Jesse Miller. He'd reduced my entire existence to a distracted, horny, frustrated, goopy mush. I'd been a hot mess all day.

Helene popped her head in the doorway. "Morning, Boss."

I barely registered her greeting as I pounded the glutinous wad in front of me with the heels of my hands.

"You okay?" she asked, her head tipping to the side, her blonde ponytail bouncing across her shoulder.

"I'm fine."

Stefanie Keefe: Dirty Rotten Liar.

Helene flipped a hand in the direction of my busywork. "Did you forget that we have a machine for that? Why are you hand-kneading that dough?"

"Working out some aggression."

Helene shrugged before becoming distracted by the box on the counter. "New shirts?" she asked, peeking inside.

"Yep."

"BAKIN' WITH BACON. Cute."

"Yep."

I grabbed my favorite rolling pin and started flattening the crust across my work surface as Helene took note of the produce crate on the wrapping table.

"Oh good!" she said. "Jesse remembered the strawberries. Who's the poor bitch that has to clean them?"

I stopped rolling and swiped a stray lock of hair from my cheek with the back of my floury hand. My eyes glazed over as I looked at the tainted box of fruit, reliving the sensual way Jesse had fed me an hour ago.

"Helloooo. Stef, you in there?"

I shook out of the vision to say, "Yes. No. What?"

Helene rolled her eyes and asked, "Do you want me to prep them or can we get Andrea to do it?"

"No, I—I'll do it."

Her nose scrunched as she asked incredulously, "You?"

My voice came out unreasonably cold as I barked, "Don't talk at me as if I don't know my way around my own kitchen, Helene. I've been covering for Becky all week and baking for my entire life prior to that."

"Whoa, take it easy, snippy! What's with you today?"

The guilt instantaneously washed over me. My mind was entirely elsewhere, but that was no excuse to go full bitch. "You're right. I'm sorry." I sighed, debating whether or not to bring my personal problems into the workplace. But ultimately, I needed a second head to help me sort out this particular problem, and Helene and I were pretty tight. "Let me ask you a question. Do you think it's possible to have a purely sexual relationship with someone?"

Helene's entire posture shifted, thrown by the sudden change in conversation. "What do you mean? Like a friends-with-benefits thing?"

"Yes, but without the friends part."

"So just a benefits situation."

"Just sex. Yes."

"Hmmm," she mused, tapping a fingertip against her chin. "I suppose so. It would depend on the people involved, right? Why? You eyeing up some new guy to be your boy toy?"

I bit my lip. "He's not new."

Helene could read me like nobody's business. "What's going on?"

I sighed, anticipating the reaction I'd be provoking by coming clean. I considered avoiding the topic entirely, but then decided to just spill it. I raised sheepish eyes to my friend and confessed, "Jesse."

Helene's eyes went wide. "Holy shit! I thought you two hated each other!"

"We kind of do."

"Oh my God. I have no idea what to say." She leaned against the counter, swiping a palm across her hair. "Hmm. I guess there *is* something to be said for grudge fucking..."

"True."

"And wow, he's totally hot."

"Also true."

She gave a shrug and laughed out, "Then what the hell? I say go for it."

* * *

It didn't necessarily take Helene to sway my thoughts on the matter, but I was happy to have the extra push to give myself the green light. It was also nice to have my opinion reinforced: *Jesse was hot.* I'd spent the past sixteen months trying not to notice, but let's be real, here. The dude was unavoidably smokin'.

I went about the rest of my morning without incident; my body was on auto-pilot even though my mind was on overdrive, trying to find a reason to talk myself out of sleeping with Jesse Miller.

There were probably a million reasons not to go through with it, but ultimately, my questions boiled down to one: *Why not live a little?*

I could do this.

It was just sex.

Nothing more.

Once my decision was made, I figured there was no need to wait. Truth be told, I was wildly excited to tell Jesse that my answer was yes.

I slipped out the front door and headed over to The Market. When I didn't see Jesse in the store, I asked his checkout girl if he had stepped out.

"Nah," Nicole said dispassionately from her post at the register, lazily picking her nails and giving a nod as she added, "He's in the back. Said he had to take care of something."

I bypassed the eyeroll and gave a quick scan through the maze of empty crates as I made my way through the stockroom. When Jesse was nowhere to be found, I figured he must've been out in the parking lot. I went to head outside, but before I reached the exit, I saw movement through the crack in the partially-opened bathroom door.

I should've known that this is what demanded Jesse's attention. The damn plumbing in this building had been a nightmare from Day One. All the store owners had complained at one time or another about the backed-up pipes that would plague us seemingly at random. I guessed it was Jesse's turn to wrestle with the plunger today.

I pushed the door open to find Jesse with his back toward me, head dropped toward the floor, one hand braced on the wall above him... the other furiously pumping away at his cock.

Oh my God!

I froze in place, shocked yet completely fascinated, watching as he strangled his meat puppet. The muscles in his arms clenched as his one hand jacked away at his massive erection, his other gripping into a white-knuckle fist against the wall. There was such strength in his powerful movements, such authority, such raw, animal sex-appeal in his every stroke. He bit his lip and dipped his head back to face the ceiling as a low growl escaped from his chest, the sound reverberating along my entire nervous system.

I knew I should have made a hasty exit, but my body refused to leave; my eyes refused to look away. I shifted from one foot to the other as my thighs rubbed together, trying to relieve the pressure building between them. I let out with a shaky breath before swallowing past the invisible obstruction in my throat.

Whatever misgivings I had about going to bed with Jesse disappeared in that instant. I knew that I wanted to fuck the hell out of that man as soon as humanly possible. I wanted every ounce of that power unleashed on me. I wanted *him*.

But before I could take even one step in his direction... his head turned and caught a glimpse of me over his shoulder.

"Shit!" he barked, trying to cover himself as best as he could, hunching over as he stuffed his dick back into his jeans.

His voice jogged me out of my trance, and I threw a hand over my eyes, obviously way too late. "Sorry!"

"Jesus, Stef. What the hell?"

I was mortified, but still had my wits about me enough to protest, "Oh, like I was supposed to know you were back here whacking it in the middle of your work day?"

I peeked through my fingers to see him zipping up as he turned toward me, an unrepentant look on his handsome face, an impressive bulge behind his jeans.

"Fine, but you see a closed door and decide to just waltz right in?"

"I thought you were clearing out the pipes!"

My bumbling comment dissolved his anger as his lip twitched, repressing a smile. "I was."

My cheeks probably blushed twelve different shades of red. "No, I meant I thought your pipes were backed up!" *Oh God, that's even worse.* "Wait. No. I was talking about the sink! I thought you were snaking the drain!"

As if my choice of words wasn't embarrassing enough, I had to go and stack my fists together and mime a plunging motion with my clenched hands. Oh my God. Why couldn't an anvil just fall on my head so I could be done with this entire conversation once and for all? I stopped jerking off the ghost penis in my grasp and slapped my hands over my reddening face, clearly mortified.

Jesse's smile broke through my humiliation. "Look. *I'm* the one who should be embarrassed here. It's not every day that I get busted, ah, *draining my snake.*" He ran a hand through his hair as he sighed, "Thing is, I kinda couldn't get my mind off our kiss from this morning. Figured I'd take care of this thing so I could get on with my day."

He was thinking of me while rubbing one out? I dropped my hands from my face as I found myself saying, "That's kind of hot."

"It's nothing compared to what I was thinking about actually doing to you."

The dangerous look on his gorgeous mug had me taking a half a step backwards. "Like what?" I asked, panicking as Jesse took two steps forward.

His lips were curled into a wicked snarl as he raised his hand and ran a thumb along my jaw. "Just say the word, Stef. Then I won't have to tell you. I can show you instead."

An electric charge ran straight down my spine at his words. The threat. The *promise*. It was totally fucking hot. "Well, that's actually why I came here," I answered tentatively, my voice cracking. "To tell you my answer is yes."

The smile he aimed in my direction made me think he wanted to devour me right then and there. If we weren't at work right at the moment, I may have let him. Besides, just knowing that Jesse was going to be in my naked grasp within a matter of hours filled me with the most delicious anticipation. I was already thrilled and excited and—okay, fine—more than a little worked up at the thought.

Jesse looked just as ecstatic. "Your place or mine?"

"Mine," I answered without hesitation. I figured I could at least regain some semblance of control if we were on my home turf. I registered his lethal gaze before turning to go, realizing a bit too late that I was in control of *nothing* about this situation. "I close at six."

CHAPTER 5

At lunchtime, I ran a bunch of necessary errands. Conveniently for me, everything I needed would be available in any of the numerous stores of our strip mall. I bought a pack of pink razors from the beauty supply before sneaking off into the bathroom to de-Sasquatch over the sink. I pit-stopped into the hair salon and had Juliet give me a quick blowout to rid my mane of its perpetual hair-tie dent. Lastly, I hit the lingerie shop and picked up a pretty bra-and-undies set (that actually matched), then stuffed my bleach-stained boulder-holder and cotton granny-panties into a Ziploc bag before stashing them away in my purse.

The rest of my workday went by at a torturous pace; a lack of customers highlighted the fact that I was a nervous, horny mess. By five-thirty, I made the decision to just send the girls home early and close up shop.

I fluffed my hair and threw on some mascara in order to look nice, but didn't go overboard with the makeover, thinking I'd appear too eager. I gave myself an assessment in the vanity mirror, pleased with the line I'd straddled between Work Me and Vixen Me... before grimacing at my boring Smoochycakes tee and jeans. There was nothing I could do about my outfit short of splurging on a new one, but I really didn't want to come off as so damned obvious. Besides, I didn't think my clothes would remain on my body for more than a few minutes anyway.

I shivered as I checked the clock, realizing that Jesse was due any minute. Thankfully, it didn't take long for inspiration to strike. I stripped down to my new black lace skivvies and pulled a pink apron off the hook, tying it over my half-naked body.

Betty Crocker meets pinup queen.

Perfect.

* * *

At six-oh-one, Jesse came tearing through my back door.

Wait. Let me rephrase that.

At six-oh-one, the back door flung open to reveal Jesse, his towering form filling its frame, a deadly smirk decorating his face. "Hey."

He was a little out of breath, and it made me wonder if he'd been anxiously watching the clock all day just as I had. I didn't get a chance to ask him because it was only about two-point-five seconds before he lunged for me.

I had no problem with that.

He fused our mouths together as my palms slid up his muscular arms, my fingertips playing under the edge of his sleeves. His lips slanted fiercely across mine, his panting breaths causing a ripple of desire to wash through me.

God, kissing Jesse felt incredible. Just his mere proximity was enough to turn me into a quivering pile of nerve endings. He took complete charge with every word, every touch, every breath. It would have been so much hotter if I could just turn my brain off and enjoy it.

But the truth was, loss of control was an alien occurrence for me. Was I truly prepared for him to lead me astray? Was I so ready and willing to give myself over to him so easily?

It was a little scary.

I tried to quiet my internal warring thoughts, but I couldn't help but wonder: How many times had he "offered his services" before?

For all the hours spent eagerly waiting for this, I was suddenly struck with a moment of hesitation. This entire situation was completely out of my wheelhouse. I was a serial monogamist; Jesse was a known man-whore. What exactly was I getting myself into?

He must have sensed my apprehension, because he pulled back, gauging my face. "What's wrong?"

"Nothing," I lied.

"You seem..."

"Hesitant?"

"Yeah."

I bit my lip as I shrugged, too embarrassed to say what I was really thinking.

Jesse pulled me to him, wrapping his arms around my body, saying, "Stef, I know I asked you not to make me wait any longer. But if you need me to, I can."

I kinda melted from his words. I mean, who knew he had it in him? "I just... I just don't want to have regrets afterward. You know?"

His lip quirked as he wrapped a strand of my hair around his finger. "Stefanie, if you let me do this, I can promise you *won't* regret it."

So damned cocky. His arrogance made me snicker and managed to change the mood between us. Relaxed. Playful.

He stepped back, finally taking a look at my outfit. "Very nice." Holding my fingertips, he ballerina-twirled me in a three-sixty to get the full picture, saying on a raised eyebrow, "Those are some expensive panties."

"What are you, a lingerie expert?"

"Yes. But that's not how I know in this particular case. There's a price tag hanging off your ass."

Dammit! I bent around at an awkward angle, locating the source of my humiliation as I gripped it in my hand. No way was I going to just rip the thing off, however. "I need scissors."

Jesse aimed an amused grin in my direction. "Just take them off."

He grabbed my fumbling hand and held it to the small of my back as he pulled me toward him, forcing my body into full-frontal contact with the length of his. He reached around me with his other hand, slowly pulling at the string of my apron. Once the knot was loosened, he released his hold to lift the garment over my head, letting it drop to the floor.

A look of pure appreciation spread across his face as his lip curled into a dangerous sneer. I stood there confidently, letting his eyes get their fill. Why the hell not, right? I spent a pretty penny on that getup and I looked damn good in it.

Jesse must have thought so, too. It was as if he couldn't control his own hands as they reached out for me, brushing his palms over my lace-covered tits, skimming his fingers down my sides. He grasped my hips and pulled me toward him again, ramming his tongue into my mouth, reaching behind me to unclasp my bra.

Jesse's practiced moves banished the last of my hesitation. I forgot to be nervous or apprehensive and simply reveled in the sensations he was stirring within me. I decided right then and there that I was his for the taking, however he wanted me. Whether it was for one single night or forever made no difference to me.

His passionate attack forced my body to bend backward at an almost ninety-degree angle, and the shivers racing along my skin were due more to his demanding kisses than the cold steel of the prep table meeting my shoulder blades. Jesse scooped his arm under my knees and lifted me to lay down on its surface, never once breaking contact with my trembling lips.

He grasped my wrists and raised them above my head, pinning my arms to the table with one of his hands. His tongue found my throat as his free hand massaged my breast until his mouth trailed down to cover one of my nipples with his hot, hungry mouth.

My cunt was throbbing as his lips moved over my skin, a heady dampness settling between my thighs. I wanted—no needed—him to touch me there, but he was too intent on prolonging the torture. He released my wrists, and my hands went automatically around his neck, pulling him to me. But he resisted, shaking his head and snickering, "You're not in control, here. I am."

He peeled my hands off his body and rested them on the table above my head again. "Don't move. Stay exactly like this for as long as I tell you, got it?"

His voice was hoarse and authoritative, and yeah, okay, totally fucking hot. I wasn't normally a girl who took orders, but the heated gaze he was aiming at me didn't dare me to disobey. I would have done anything he asked of me in that moment. And he knew it.

So, I lay there, completely free to defy him, but instead, I followed his command. My hands gripped the edge of the table above my head as my tits arched toward him; my knees bent slightly. He took a leisurely perusal down my body, so seductive it felt as if his hands were caressing me instead of his eyes. His gaze travelled over my naked flesh, his face moving closer to the skin at my shoulder. He never touched me. Just breathed along my prone form from my neck down to my toes. Inhaling me, then blowing soft whispers of air against my skin, causing me to lose my mind. My fingers were itching to touch him; my cunt was throbbing, practically begging to feel his hot cock inside me; my pulse was racing with anticipation. It was the sweetest torture I'd ever endured.

His voice broke through my daze. "I brought something. Hope you're okay with it."

A long silk scarf was pulled from his back pocket and dangled in front of my eyes. He wasted no time before dancing it along my skin, kissing it down my hip, over my ankles, up my legs, flitting across my damp clit. Even that whisper of contact had me exploding out of my skin, and I bit my lip as I tightened my fists on the edge of the table in a white-knuckle grip.

Jesse wrapped the scarf around my wrists in such a skilled manner that his practiced movements managed to come off as almost... graceful. The thought was short-lived, however. An evil grin decorated his gorgeous face as he pulled downward—fiercely—and tied the ends of the scarf to the support bar under the table. My back arched at an almost uncomfortable angle but it felt so good, so good.

He grasped me firmly by the ankles, and I wondered if he'd be tying those up, too. As if reading my mind, he scolded, "Not today. I want to feel your legs wrapped around me while I make you come." With that, he forced my feet dangerously apart, splaying my legs wide open. I was laid bare for his perusal and God only knows what else he had planned. I felt the wetness trickle down into the crack of my ass, and my heart was beating so fast, I thought I'd pass out.

He was a mad scientist, hovering over the specimen lain out on his examining table. Holy shit, after we were through defiling this thing, I was going to need to call in the hazmat team.

He reached into a bin on the shelf above me and came up with a handful of powdered sugar, sprinkling a dusting of white across my chest. "Beautiful. Just like I pictured. All tied up and even sweeter than usual." He waggled his eyebrows as he added, "Sugar Tits..."

I would have laughed, but Jesse's tongue had already made its way to the skin of my breast, lightly licking, tasting, before closing his mouth over its tip... and clamping his teeth on my nipple. The bite shot an electric current straight between my thighs, pain and pleasure all mixed into one. He slid his fingers over my navel, down to my inner thighs, down one, up the other, over my hip... dancing around the one spot I so desperately wanted him to touch, teasing me. I thought I'd explode before he ever got inside me.

And then—finally—he ghosted a fingertip over my clit. The contact almost had me bursting right then and there. He added increasing pressure as he rubbed the sensitive spot, his movements becoming more intense, my nerve endings seconds from imploding. *Oh God. Oh God yes.* I was so close... so close...

And then he stopped.

My throat let out with an involuntary groan of protest, causing him to chuckle. "Patience, Sugar."

I struggled against the restraints, feeling I was going mad. No use. The guy knew his way around a slipknot. I was left with no choice but to lay there, completely impatient and frustrated.

He pulled off his shirt and I was blessed with a glimpse of that magnificent body, his lean muscles bunching under his smooth skin. I watched— mesmerized—as he unbuttoned his jeans and let them drop to the floor. I wasn't aware that Jesse was in the military, but apparently he was a high-ranking commando. Boom.

After he rolled on the condom, he wrapped his hand around his massive dick and started fucking his palm, a lethal smile on his gorgeous face as he snarked, "I know you like to watch."

His impressive meat javelin came to life in his hands as he stroked it, never taking his eyes off mine.

Jesse climbed on top of the table and covered my naked body with his own. Just the feel of his skin against mine set my nerves on fire, the sight of him on top of me too spectacular to comprehend. He rubbed his cock over my clit, my head thrashing from side to side, my limbs straining against the restraints, groaning, begging, *"Please."*

In one forceful movement, he slammed himself inside of me. My entire body tensed at the invasion, his thick cock stretching me to my limits, the throbbing, pulsing ache inside my body as my cunt protested and loved it all at once. I forgot how much I loved sex. The closeness. The abandon. The *want*.

His hands gripped the edge of the table above my head, using it for leverage as he pulled himself deeper into me, and before long, he was pounding away at my aching hole again and again and again. My entire existence was reduced to the assault of rigid steel, both at my back and between my legs. Every thrust exuded power, his greedy cock taking and giving all at once.

I loved the feel of his hips grinding against mine—punishing, forceful, demanding—fucking me hot, dirty, hard. And still, it wasn't enough. It wasn't nearly enough.

"Harder," I begged like a wanton whore, surprised that the word had even slipped from my mouth.

But Jesse heeded the demand, his guttural moaning against my neck serving as a battle cry as he complied, slamming inside of me, raw, sweaty, choking on his words as he scratched out, "Fuck, you're so wet. So fucking tight."

He rammed his tongue in my mouth as he fucked me hard, almost painfully, his thrusts pounding away at my body, his hips crashing against mine as I lay helpless, bound in place, at his mercy.

I wrapped my legs around him, crossing my ankles over the small of his back, locking his body to mine. I wanted to touch him. It wasn't fair that he was having all the fun. Well, not *all* the fun. My pink parts were doing a happy dance as the base of his cock rubbed against my clit on every thrust, bringing me closer, closer, building, building...

The orgasm hit me hard and fast, detonating my nerve endings in a cataclysmic implosion. "Oh God!" I screamed as my back arched off the table, my insides shattering into a million pieces.

My response made him smirk, looking rather proud of himself as he rocked faster, harder, seeking his own release. I was deaf, dumb, and blind by that point, but still managed to clench my muscles around his demanding cock. The increased tightness pushed Jesse completely over the edge as he grabbed the table in his tormented clutches and pulled himself into me rough and rapid and deep before letting out with a booming growl, grinding himself into me for a final thrust as his cock pulsed incessantly inside of me, draining the both of us.

He collapsed on top of my naked body with a laughing groan as he reached his wasted arms up to untie the knots at my wrists, setting me free. I was surprised to find my arms wrapping around his shoulders, pulling him tightly to me as he continued to fuck me slowly with his softening dick. I didn't ever want him to pull out of me. I wanted to lay there like that forever, the two of us joined in sweaty, post-coital bliss for all eternity. Jesse wasn't in any hurry to leave our position either.

But soon enough and against my will, the real world crept back in.

Jesse pulled out and went about the task of cleaning himself up. "How you doing there, Cupcake?"

I was still trying to catch my breath as I let out with an elated, "Good. Great, actually!"

Jesse grinned in response. "Yeah, me too. I never knew you were such a wildcat. Glad to see you're open to some adventure."

"What? The tying-up thing?"

"Yeah. I guess you could say you passed my test."

"I'm not sure how to feel about that."

"Don't worry; you were everything I hoped you'd be and more."

"Yeah, but—"

He shushed me with his mouth before pulling back to explain, "I just needed to know if you'd be open to this kind of stuff."

"What stuff? Like S&M stuff?"

He started to chuckle. "Sugar, no. The kind of things I'm into barely scratch the surface of that world. I like a bit of kink; I'm not looking to beat the shit out of you. I'm a control freak, not a sadist."

"How so?"

"A little light bondage, some toys, a bit of Dom play. Nothing too crazy."

I mulled that over. It didn't seem like anything I couldn't handle. "Fine. But next time, don't test me. *Ask.* Okay?"

"Okay. You're right. I guess I didn't think to ask because a scarf hardly counts as kink. I was only easing you in. I won't make that mistake again."

If tying me up was "easing me in," I couldn't even imagine what other tricks this guy had up his sleeve. Because yeah. If our future encounters were even close to what I experienced today, I was totally game.

CHAPTER 6

The next morning, I was confused about how I should act toward Jesse. I didn't know how often I could expect to take him up on his "offer." Based on how we talked about it after our first encounter, I was pretty confident we weren't going to limit our arrangement to a single night of debauchery. But did that mean we were going to be exclusive? For how long? Did it mean we'd hook up every day? Once a week? Every month? I'm ashamed to admit that I was actually hoping for more of an *hourly*-type schedule.

He was at his door as usual when I pulled into the back lot. As I got out of the car, I fiddled with my keys on my walk toward him, and couldn't help but notice the sly smile he was aiming at me.

"Hey Sweet Cheeks, want me to unlock that back door for you?" he asked.

There was nothing to do but drop my head and chuckle. Jesse laughed too as he added, "I made a full pot of coffee. Why don't you drop off your stuff then come over?"

"Sounds good. Just give me a minute."

By the time I got everything situated at the bakery and popped over to The Market, Jesse was unloading some peppers onto their spot in a display bin. His strong, muscular arm was holding a wooden crate against his hip as he worked, and I found myself getting a bit sweaty and keyed up as I watched those talented hands in action. The same hands that had turned me to mush the night before.

The bastard didn't even look up as he asked, "Enjoying the view?"

I decided to just be honest. "Yes, actually."

He winked as I stepped closer and leaned against the produce bin next to him.

"Mine's bigger," he said, nodding his head in the direction of my hands and ohmygod I was absently stroking the cucumbers. I was flustered and embarrassed, but Jesse just snickered as he offered, "If you want to add playthings into our sessions, that can be arranged."

I was intrigued. "What do you mean? Like what?"

He shrugged. "I can easily walk down to Drew's and grab us something fun..."

Drew owned the novelty shop a few stores down. Along with the gag gifts and blacklight posters, he had an entire "adult" section of the store devoted to sex toys and vintage porno DVDs. "Oh dear Lord, no. I caught a glimpse of that horror show one time and now my brain can't unsee it."

He put the crate on the floor, stepped closer, and looped his arms around my waist. "We'll work our way up to it."

"Oh we will, will we?" I laughed out, smiling as I let him kiss me.

And that small contact was all it took. Before I knew it, I was clawing at his shirt. He took the cue and fisted his hand behind his shoulder blades, stripping off his tee before pulling mine over my head and undoing my bra. I palmed his length and found that he was already hard. *Nice.*

We both worked the buttons and zippers at our jeans, ripping them down our legs quickly as he spun me around and started to bend me over the heirloom tomatoes.

"Oh God eww no!" I protested. "Not on the food, for chrissakes!"

"Shit. You're right. I just got those in and they were fucking expensive. Can't afford to throw them all out."

He directed my naked form a few steps over to the front counter, spun me away from him, and forced my head down to bend over its surface as he put on a condom. My hands wrapped around the edge of the counter, causing Jesse to say, "Oh, Sugar. You should see how hot you look right now. So perfect. Just like that. Don't move a muscle."

Not that I could. In this position, my torso was practically immobilized next to the cash register. Poor Nicole would be working in this spot all day, having no idea what debauchery took place here mere hours before.

He tore my undies down to my ankles, grabbed my hair in his fist, and slapped my ass. *What the hell?* I shot him a warning look over my shoulder as his brows raised, gauging my reaction, asking for permission. "You like it when I spank you?"

God help me, I totally did. "I do."

"Does it hurt?"

"Just a little," I answered, bypassing the confession about how good it felt, too.

"Should I kiss it and make it better?"

Better? I was already seconds away from climaxing right there next to the counter display of Halvah bars. "Yes."

Jesse immediately dropped to his knees and buried his face in my ass. His fingers dug into the flesh of my butt cheeks as he licked the space in between. My legs almost gave out from the delicious sensations he was stirring inside me, and that was even before he pressed the tip of his tongue against my sensitive skin, forcing his way inside. Holy shit, he was tongue-fucking my asshole, and hell if it didn't feel incredible. Then again, I guess I shouldn't have been surprised that the produce guy from Rimmer knew how to toss a proper salad.

It felt like an eternity before he finally came up for air. He stood, pressing his hips against my backside to say, "My dick is so hard right now. You want me to fuck you?"

The guy wasn't lying. It felt like a titanium flagpole back there prodding the flesh of my butt. I was more than ready myself. "Yes."

He smacked my ass again. "Tell me. Tell me you want my cock inside you."

"I thought I just did," I managed.

Smack! "You're gonna need to do better than that. Beg me."

"I want it."

Smack! He leaned over and hissed against my ear, *"I said beg."*

Holy hell. Was he the hottest thing ever or what? "I want your big cock inside me. Please. Please fuck me."

Jesse positioned himself between my legs, and with one demanding shove, he was in. He grabbed my shoulders for leverage and pulled himself into me deep, pounding against me in a forceful rhythm. It felt phenomenal, being taken so roughly by a man who knew what he was doing. My tits smashed against the hard Formica counter with every thrust. The line between pain and pleasure had been blurred, and all I knew was that I loved every minute of it.

I removed one of my hands to brush the hair out of my eyes and got smacked again. "I told you *not* to let go of that counter."

It was so hot to hear his normally smooth voice oozing with authority. I was learning that it was his bedroom voice, the one he used exclusively while we were fooling around, to wield control, to overpower me in the very best possible way. I hadn't realized I could be so compliant, but I loved how he took charge. I loved giving myself over to him, trusting him to bring me to places I'd never been before. And that lack of inhibition made for the most incredible sex I've ever experienced in my life.

His dick was hammering into me in a punishing cadence, so I almost didn't notice as his thumb slid down the crack of my ass, pushing at the tight opening. There was no argument from me as he used my own wetness to lube my asshole and pressed his finger inside. *Oh my God.* I almost came right at that very second. Between his massive beef-bat pumping inside my pink canoe and his finger filling my starfruit... it was too much. The pressure. The overwhelming feeling of fullness. It heightened every sensation inside me.

And then he added his gravelly voice to the equation. "I'm going to fuck you here, too. You ever been fucked in the ass?"

Holy shit! I was teetering on the edge of an apocalyptic orgasm, but I managed to answer him. "No."

He slammed into me deeper, landing another smack on my backside. "Say it."

"I've never been fucked there."

"Tell me you're going to let me fuck your virgin asshole."

My cunt started to convulse at his words; my entire body throbbing. I was wound too tight. Oh God I was going to—*"Oh fuck! Ohhh God! Yes!"* My torso thrashed uncontrollably as I came, my ass bucking back against his demanding cock. His hands grabbed my hips as he pounded himself into me with a force that actually hurt and felt amazing at the same time, fucking me hard and deep and fast until he exploded with a fantastic roar, the both of us collapsing onto the carpet in a breathless, panting, sweaty heap of flesh.

My entire body was on fire; my mind was a discombobulated mess. So I wasn't exactly in the right headspace when Jesse said, "We really need to stop doing this."

My stomach dropped suddenly at his words, throwing my brain into a panic. *Stop? What does he mean, stop? We just started!*

He pulled me tighter against his side, adding, "We can't keep fucking at work. Let me take you to bed."

Phew. "Okay," I answered casually, even while feeling anything but. I was still reeling from the overwhelming thought that he was done with me. Thank God that wasn't the case. "Whose?"

His wicked grin made me wonder what further depravity was in store for me. "Mine."

CHAPTER 7

Jesse and I didn't get too many opportunities to socialize over the course of our day, and thankfully, the store was so busy that it managed to distract me appropriately. But after closing, I was able to focus solely on my night ahead.

The first order of business was to pit-stop home to shower and put on something pretty. Jesse only ever saw me in my work attire, which normally warranted nothing more than a Smoochycakes tee and jeans. But that night, I poured myself into a lethal white dress that was tight enough to border on obscene. Meh. What the hell. "Obscene" was most likely going to be the order for the evening anyhow.

I lost the ponytail, took an obnoxiously long time to style my hair, and actually put on a full face of makeup. It had been so long since I got all dolled up that I'd almost forgotten how, but dammit if the end result wasn't entirely worth it.

The plan was that he would make "a proper Sunday dinner" and I'd be in charge of dessert. So, I grabbed the cake that I'd made at work earlier in the day and headed out to my Jeep. I punched his address into my GPS and followed the directions to his house, only an eight-minute drive away. His home was a modest brown ranch, a non-descript, cookie-cutter rectangle that matched every other house on the street. Very suburban. Not exactly where I would have ever pictured a guy like Jesse to live. It was cute, though.

Jesse answered the door looking delicious, of course. He was wearing a pair of dark jeans and a yellow, button-down shirt with the sleeves rolled to his elbows. Yum.

"Well, hello, gorgeous," he said, opening the door wide and grinning even wider as he gave me a quick peck on the cheek. The scruff at his jaw tickled my skin as I caught a whiff of his clean, soapy scent.

The space immediately to the right of the small foyer was his dining room, and I took note of the set table and lit candles, nodding my head, impressed. "Nice digs."

"Thanks. I've only been here a few months and you're my first visitor."

Unlikely. I didn't know what to say to that. "I brought goodies," I said, holding up the cake platter. "Chekhov Lemon Chiffon."

At Smoochycakes, we always put a spin on traditional recipes. This one had layers of fluffy angel food with a lemon custard filling, slathered in white buttercream and coated in shredded coconut. This was not your mother's lemon chiffon.

I uncovered the cake and placed it on the serving buffet as Jesse came up behind me, wrapping his arms around my waist. "Can't wait to taste your goodies, Sugar."

He gave my neck a quick nuzzle before leading me toward the back of the house to the kitchen. Everything smelled divine.

"Mmm. Yum. Whatcha making?" I asked.

Jesse poured me a glass of cabernet as he answered, "I've got steaks in the broiler and some mashed potatoes in the warming tray, but right now, I'm getting ready to chop some vegetables for the salad."

I hopped up onto the counter, grabbed a raw carrot from the cutting board, and took a bite. "Can I do anything?"

He leered at me, answering playfully, "Like I'm letting you anywhere near this hand-picked, work-of-art produce."

My eyes tightened, meeting his hungry gaze. "Oh, I'd like to think I know what I'm doing when it comes to your... *produce*," I taunted. And then, I boldly slid the carrot into my mouth. Slowly. Deep.

Jesse's expression was the picture of aching lust, pain drifting across his features. Ha! Awesome.

"You tease. You think I won't let this entire meal burn just to test you on that?"

"I really hope you won't. I'm starving."

The glare he aimed at me was positively ravenous. "So am I." He turned off the burners and unzipped his pants. "Do it again."

I almost choked as he pulled out his already-hard cock and started fucking his hand. But I kept up with the show, sliding the carrot between my lips, sucking on it earnestly, letting him see what I really wanted to do to *him*. He couldn't take his eyes off of my mouth as he pumped his shaft, and it turned me on so bad that my cunt was absolutely aching at the sight. Just to further the torture, I bent my legs and placed my heels on the counter, giving him an all-access view of the silky white panties I was wearing under my skirt.

Stefanie Keefe: Uninhibited Slut.

Jesse's head dropped in agony as a painful groan rumbled from his throat. He stepped closer and slid my soaked panties to the side, immediately plunging two fingers into my wet hole. I gasped at the invasion and deep-throated the carrot as payback. He speared me hard and stroked my clit, instantaneously causing a category-five hurricane to ravage my insides. I moaned as I pressed myself against his palm, wanting to feel him deeper, harder. Jesse kept up the pace, finger-fucking me relentlessly with one hand while jacking himself off with the other, and I knew I wouldn't be able to hold out much longer.

As in, not at all.

I screamed as I came, my hot cunt convulsing around his deft fingers, soaking his hand. My lungs were exhausted, my legs felt like Jell-O, and the most delectable aftershocks were still tingling down my spine. I swiped the hair off my sweaty brow as Jesse sucked me off his fingertips, a move which almost had me climaxing all over again.

His eyes darkened dangerously as his lids dropped to half-mast. "Those pretty lips sucking on that carrot... *Oh fuck*, will they look that good around my cock?"

I caught my breath and repressed my smile to say, "Maybe we should find out."

Jesse was in obvious agony. God, it was so fun to tease him. "On your knees."

Every inch of my skin started buzzing at the command. So hot. I dropped down in front of him as he shoved his pants down to his ankles and slipped his third leg between my waiting lips. My breathing was choppy around his massive girth, but I took him in eagerly, devouring him with delirious gusto as his hips rocked back and forth, matching my enthusiasm with his own.

"Such a vision," he scratched out. "So pretty, you on your knees sucking me off."

Knowing that I was giving him such pleasure almost turned me on more than the things he'd just done to me a few minutes ago. I couldn't tell him that, however. A certain obstruction was currently preventing me from speaking.

"You like when I fuck your mouth, Sugar?"

To tell you the truth, I totally did. My cheeks suctioned around his dick as I looked up at him with eager, wide eyes, shook my head in the affirmative, and took him deeper.

His voice caught as he asked through gravel, *"You like it rough?"*

He was starting to lose it. *Nice.* I gripped his ass in my hands and pulled him toward me in answer, and that was about all he could take. A growl rumbled through his chest as he grabbed me by my hair and slammed his cock to the back of my throat. My mouth was starting to cramp up; my eyes were tearing from the invasion. I loved every minute of it.

"Oh fuck. You're so fucking hot right now. You're gonna make me come."

I cupped his tightened balls in my palm and pressed a fingertip against his asshole, same as he'd done to me that morning. That little move sent Jesse completely over the edge, and trust me when I tell you that it was a thing of beauty. I couldn't help but groan around his cock as he started pumping himself into me at a furious pace. I thought I was going to choke from his violent thrusts but I managed to take it. I managed to love it.

"So close, so close..."

Beads of sweat gathered at his forehead as he tightened his fists in my hair and jacked his hips one final time, letting out with a primal roar. Hot cum spurted to the back of my throat, and I swallowed with more enthusiasm than I would have thought possible. But as it turned out, *everything* about Jesse Miller was delectable, even his ball batter. I swirled my tongue around the tip of his yogurt-slinger as I sucked the last of his release.

Stefanie Keefe: Cock-Gobbling Thundercunt.

"Holy shit," he said, trying to catch his breath and grinning like a deviant. "I'm never going to look at a carrot the same way again."

I laughed as I got up from the floor and went to the bathroom to clean up.

Finding myself with a few minutes of solace allowed my brain to regain function. I looked in the mirror, almost not recognizing the uninhibited sex goddess looking back at me. *What have I become?* I knew taking Jesse up on his "offer" wasn't supposed to be about anything more than sex. And I went into this situation with my eyes wide open, in complete accord with our arrangement, not expecting anything more. At least I understood how he managed to get as many girls as he did. Jesse emitted sex at every turn. I tried to deny his appeal for upwards of an entire year, but I knew all along that sex with him was an inevitability. But the idea that I was just another one of Jesse's whores kept niggling at the back of my mind, and I wasn't sure that I liked how it felt.

Then again... maybe we were more than just fuck buddies. It was hard to believe when he said I was the first person to visit his lair, but I got the impression he was telling me the truth.

What did that say about us? We saw each other at work every day, so I guess you could say we'd kind of been friends for the past sixteen months, try as I might
to deny it. And now, here we were, getting ready to sit down and share a meal together. Being in his house suddenly felt like we were... *dating*. What else can you call it?

CHAPTER 8

I was quiet as I came back out to the kitchen, but Jesse's busywork kept him from noticing. He plated our steaks as I grabbed the sides, hauling everything to the dining room and depositing the dishes on the table.

I placed my napkin across my lap as Jesse filled my plate. "I'm impressed, Mr. Miller. Everything looks fantastic!"

"It sure does, Ms. Keefe," he replied through a smirk. I cursed the heat rising in my cheeks as he readied his own plate and took his seat.

I loaded my fork with some salad and took a bite. Delicious. "Are these the heirloom tomatoes?"

"Yep."

"I'm kind of glad we didn't defile them this morning. They're really good!"

"What can I say? Produce is my life. Believe it or not, I do know how to run my business."

His pronouncement reminded me of our conversation from yesterday. "Yes, you certainly do." I cleared my throat before steering him back toward the subject of Smoochycakes. "In fact, it would seem you know *my* business, too."

Jesse put his fork down and looked at me cautiously. "I wasn't trying to insult you when I said that, you know."

"No, I know. I'm actually curious to hear your ideas."

"Oh, I've got ideas, Sugar," he said, sliding a deadly perusal along my person.

I couldn't help but snicker. The guy had such a one-track mind. "About the *bakery*, Jesse."

He chuckled. "Stef, I already told you. The *bakery* needs *you* working your magic in that kitchen. God, the stuff you used to come up with. What were those titty cookies you used to make?"

"Titty cookies?"

"Yeah, the ones that looked like tits. The chocolate ones."

I started laughing. The "titties" were nothing more than Hershey's kisses nestled in a chocolate-peanut-butter dough. I guess they did look like boobs. "Do you mean *Biddies?*"

"Yeah! Those were awesome. Why'd you stop making those?"

Biddies were my grandmother's recipe. I'd been baking those things my entire life—and they were yummy—so of course I put them on Smoochycakes' menu. But after I left the kitchen, we had to take them out of the lineup. "I didn't want to share my grandmother's secret recipe, so I was the only one who could make them. I guess I just didn't have the time anymore."

"Well, there you go. That's kind of what I was trying to tell you. No one you hire is going to have your passion. *You* were the one that made everything delicious," he said, eyeing me appreciatively.

He was right about my "passion." I did love to bake. Shame that I didn't get much chance to do so, but that was only because I couldn't be a baker and a store manager at the same time.

And that was the moment that the answer to my problem suddenly became crystal clear: *I'm a baker.* I'd been such a control freak about the wrong thing, been delegating the wrong job. It was such a simple solution to hand over the office and take back my kitchen. It was exciting to think about.

I'd already come to the conclusion about what I needed to do, but now I just needed to act. I leaned across the table conspiratorially and winked. "Know anyone who's good with numbers?"

Jesse smiled, pleased to see that I was taking his advice to heart. "How is it that a beautiful girl like you is still single?"

My brain was already busily figuring out the logistics of revamping my entire business, so his question caught me off guard. I almost choked on my mouthful of steak. I swallowed hard before answering, "Single *again*, you mean."

"Uh oh. Sounds like there's a story there."

I shrugged, twirling my fork through my mashed potatoes. "Yes, but not a *new* one, I'm afraid." When Jesse stayed silent, I added, "Girl meets boy. Girl marries boy. Boy proceeds to fuck everything with a pulse."

Jesse leaned back in his chair, scrutinizing me. "You're a woman with a past."

"*Every* woman has a past."

"I'm not interested in other women."

Ha! Yeah right! "Jesse, I'm perfectly willing to talk about myself, but please don't pretend that I'm so unique when I do. We both know what your deal is."

"My *deal?*"

Talking about my ex reminded me that I was currently sitting across the table from yet another man-whore, and I started to fire up. Would I ever learn? "Yes. Your deal regarding your complete aversion to monogamy."

"My *deal* is that you have no idea what you're talking about. My *deal* is that I got burned once, too. You don't hold the patent on broken egos, Stef."

Interesting that he didn't say "broken hearts." Because that was the thing: My ex hadn't broken my heart. He'd broken my *spirit*. Jesse was able to recognize that I was a wrecked woman, apparently because he'd been hurt once, too. It was an unspoken ability of damaged people to find each other. It's like we could sniff out any fellow humans who were also carrying around their own ton of extra baggage. I'd sensed this in Jesse from the start, but never had a serious enough conversation with him in order to explore it.

When I returned nothing but a silent gaze, he explained, "Five years. High school sweethearts. She kept pushing to get engaged; I felt we were too young. Finally had a big blowout about it, where I learned she'd been screwing her boss for the past eight months. They ended up moving to Florida together. I haven't seen her since. And yeah, it fucking sucked."

His confession calmed me down a bit, especially once I registered genuine hurt in his eyes. "I'm sorry."

"Don't be. Misty obviously wasn't the right girl for me. I'm a one-woman kind of guy and I don't like to share. I'm sure you think that I've just been screwing everything in my path for the past six years to run from my feelings. So, yeah. You want to judge me for going full-slut after that? Go ahead. But you'd be wrong." His eyebrow dipped as he added, "The fact is, my whoring around had nothing to do with feelings about my *ex*."

I didn't know what he was getting at, but was unsettled by that small taste of his squishy cream filling. I didn't like to let my guard down when it came to Jesse Miller; it was easier to have a no-strings arrangement when I could think of him as nothing more than my sex-idiot. But there he was, exposing the chink in his armor, reminding me that he was an actual person with actual feelings.

It made me like him even more, and I wasn't sure how I felt about it.

I bypassed the interrogation and changed the subject instead. "So, um, the steaks are perfect."

Jesse collected his thoughts in the extra beat it took for him to respond. "Thanks. I can only take so much credit. Pete's the one who suggested this cut."

"Who's Pete?"

"The new guy. Runs the butcher shop a few stores down. You haven't met him yet?"

My eyes tightened as I tried to place him. "He the scruffy hottie with the shaggy hair?"

Jesse lowered a brow in my direction. "Don't test me."

His reaction caught me by surprise. I tried not to laugh as I sputtered out, "Holy crap. Are you *jealous?*"

"Not hardly."

Regardless of what Jesse said, I could tell that he was full of it. His envious response had me revisiting the questions I'd been asking myself earlier. "Hey Jesse?" I started in cautiously. "What exactly is this?"

Jesse stopped chewing, looking at me as if I'd grown a second head. "Dinner."

"No. I meant what are we doing? What is *this?*" I asked, motioning my finger between him and me.

Jesse's head dropped as his shoulders sank. He mumbled to his plate, but I was still able to make out his words: "Twenty. Four. Hours."

"Huh?"

He looked up to meet my eyes, a smarmy tone in his voice as he answered, "Congratulations. That's a new record."

"What is? What are you talking about?"

Jesse put down his fork and leaned back in his chair, eyeing me impatiently. "Stef. We've been fucking for exactly one day and you're already asking me *relationship* questions?"

"Oh my God, no! I didn't mean—"

"Sure as hell sounds like it."

Of course it sounded like I was fishing for a label. But only because *he'd* been throwing out mixed signals since Day One. "I was just wondering, I mean, I thought we were just going to be having lots of crazy sex. But now we're talking about our personal lives... with steaks on our plates... dessert waiting for us... This just seems an awful lot like a date."

"I like you, I like to eat, and I like to fuck. That's all there is to it. If you've got a problem with any of those things, the door's right there."

I couldn't get a read on his tone. It was as if his words and his voice didn't align. Was this another test? "What a douchey thing to say."

"Pardon?"

"Douchey. As in, spoken like a douchebag."

"Well," he said menacingly, "since you think I'm such a *douche*, what the hell are you still doing here?"

Not one minute ago, I was getting all melty and gooey from seeing his vulnerable side. The dude could be hella charming when he really wanted to be.

He could also be blunt and insulting.

I stood up, slapping my napkin to the table as I spat out, "It's been a *fabulous* night, but I really *ought* to be going."

Jesse almost knocked over his chair in his dash to the front door. He whipped it open and gave an intimation of a stately bow. "But of course, *madame*. And make a point to lose my address, will ya?"

"Gladly!" I started to stomp out of the room when I saw my lemon chiffon sitting on the serving buffet. *Fuck him if he thinks he'll ever get a taste of my "goodies" ever again.* "And I'm taking my cake with me, asshole!"

I grabbed the platter off the server with all intentions of going home, planting my ass on my couch with a fork, and eating the whole thing by myself. He didn't deserve any of it.

On second thought...

Before I was fully aware of what I was doing... I smashed the thing right into his smarmy face.

We both froze in that second, the two of us in disbelief about what I'd just done. The aluminum platter fell to the floor along with the bulk of the mashed cake as Jesse wiped a sizable chunk of it off his face. And then his fingers swiped across his eyes to reveal two malicious chips of brimstone, staring me down in a lethal glare.

Oh shit!

I figured I'd better make a run for it. But before I could, Jesse squished a cake-covered hand into my hair.

"You *bastard!*" I spat, as bits of lemon custard dripped down my face.

Jesse looked rather pleased with himself as he flicked his other hand in my general direction, landing a splat of gooey frosting against my middle.

I had cake dripping into my eyes, but for some reason, it was that splotch on my new white dress that made me snap.

My hand sliced through the air on its own, itching to make contact with his smirking face. But it was stopped on its way to its intended target when Jesse grabbed my wrist in a sticky vice. His hand tightened as we stared each other down—our teeth bared, our chests heaving—until I caught a glimmer of mischief behind those topaz orbs. He was *enjoying* this!

My brain was a frantic jumble, trying to come up with a scathing remark... when I suddenly found myself slamming against his body and crashing our lips together.

Lemon custard smushed between us as our mouths clashed viciously. Angel food and buttercream squished between my fingers as my hands knotted into his hair. Jesse's frosting-covered hand grabbed at my breast as his other palm smeared up my thigh, palming my ass and pulling me into direct contact with his hardening cock.

I was breathless and infuriated and completely covered in decimated baked goods.

Oh, and also... incredibly turned on.

I dropped to my knees and undid his zipper, pulling him out and coating his thick cock with frosting from my hand before sliding my mouth over him. I licked his girth clean, sucking every trace of buttercream from his sweet stick.

"Does it taste good?" he asked. "You like to lick my cock?"

I moaned around it, answering, "Mm hmm."

He dropped to the floor over the cake mess and pulled me on top of his body to straddle him. My knees squished into the slippery goo as I stripped off his sticky shirt and smeared it across his chest, finger-painting his beautiful bumpy abs with pulverized cake before dropping my head to lick it off.

My mouth moved back to his as my silky panties rubbed against his bare cock, and Jesse grasped my hips to increase the friction, aggressively rocking himself into me.

There was a tortuous rumble vibrating in his chest as he bit my bottom lip, gave me a sharp smack against my ass, and announced, "My turn, Sugar. I want to suck your tits."

He rolled us both over and pulled my dress over my head, grabbed a handful of cake from the abandoned platter and slapped it to my chest before licking the frosting from my breasts.

It felt naughty and delightful, but I wasn't able to get caught up in the ministrations of his talented tongue. Angry fucks were great, but wouldn't change the fact that we still had some stuff to sort out.

"Hey Jesse?" I asked warily. "I think maybe we should talk first."

He popped his mouth off my nipple and traced a finger around its rim. "About what?"

"About the fact that you were a bit of a dick."

He stopped and met my eyes. "I know. I'm sorry. I get a little defensive whenever it comes to relationship talk."

"I wasn't trying to get you to declare your intentions or—"

"I know you weren't. I freaked out anyway."

"I get it. I appreciate the explanation. And truly, I'm sorry, too."

His lip curled into a roguish grin as his eyes tightened on mine, teasing. He planted a quick suction-kiss on my boob before changing the subject. "Mmm. I think I need to get you in the shower."

"Yes, please!"

We were chuckling as he stood and hauled me to my feet, allowing me to assess the damage. We were both covered in cake and his floor was a disaster. Thank God for tile.

I grimaced at my once-beautiful work of art, now an unrecognizable smush. "I worked hard on that, dammit." I gestured a hand along my body from head to toe as I added, "On this, too, for that matter."

Jesse led me down the hall, shooting a deadly grin over his shoulder as he slithered, "And. Both. Were. Delicious."

CHAPTER 9

Jesse's bathroom was pretty huge, decorated in dark gray marble. A large, glass-enclosed shower area took over a sizeable portion of the far wall, and it was there that we stripped off the last of our sticky clothes.

Jesse ran the water, and it spewed from all directions, quickly steaming the glass. He ran a finger across my collarbone, swiping a smudge of buttercream off my skin and placing it on his tongue. "Just one last taste..."

He slipped an arm around my waist and pulled our naked bodies together to brand his mouth to mine, walking me backwards into the shower stall. My back pressed against the cool tile wall as he kissed me into oblivion, the hot water saturating every inch of my skin.

I was starting to get a little too used to this.

Just the mere proximity of Jesse Miller was enough to get my heart racing; a simple kiss was enough to throw my entire world into a tailspin. I'd never experienced anything like this. I knew our "relationship" wasn't supposed to be about anything more than sex, but when he held me like this—with his arms wrapped around me so tight, sending warmth across my skin—it was hard to remember I wasn't supposed to be falling in love with him.

At least now I knew better than to try and tell him that, however.

He separated our lips and turned me toward a spray of water, allowing me to rinse my body from head to toe. Jesse deposited a dollop of shampoo into his palm and massaged it into my hair, working his fingers across my scalp with intimate care, and I leaned back against him, purring like a kitten. "Mmm. That feels amazing," I mewled, closing my eyes and getting lost in his pampering.

"Oh yeah?" he snickered. "Just wait until I start in with the soap."

I giggled as I turned to face him, dipping my head back into the flow of water and rinsing the suds from my hair. I don't want to overhype the situation or anything, but I totally porned it up. How often would I ever find myself in the position to put on a sex show? I closed my eyes and tipped my head back, lifting my arms to swipe the hair from my face, jutting my chest toward Jesse, the suds slipping between my tits.

He took the bait, grasping my breasts in his hands and closing his mouth over one of them. The water rushed over us both, and let me tell you, the showerhead wasn't the only thing hot and dripping at that moment.

Jesse kissed his way over my shoulder, stepping behind me, cupping my tits in his hands as he sucked at my neck, peppering hot kisses across my skin. I reached behind me to pull his head in closer as his hips pressed into my backside, his hot, hard dick sliding along the crack of my ass.

"You gonna let me fuck you here?" he asked, pressing the tip of his peen right up against my balloon knot.

"Mmm. Maybe," I teased.

"I seem to remember you *begging* me to do it this morning..."

I snickered. "I can't be held responsible for the things I agree to while mid-orgasm."

"Well, now that you have your wits about you," he said, sliding his soapy fingers across my clit, "can I get a definitive yes?"

I started rocking against the motion of his hand, reveling in the little earthquakes he was encouraging in my belly, loving the sweet pressure of his cock nudging against my back door. It already felt pretty amazing, but I was understandably a little hesitant. "Will it hurt?" I asked.

"Not if we do it right."

I was uneasy about it, but mostly, I was curious. Jesse had already taken me to places I'd never been before, why not let him visit a place *no one else* had ever been before? Before I could fully explore the thought, my mouth answered on its own. "Okay."

He slid his hands up my arms, raising them over my head, grasping my wrists and pressing his body against me, flattening the length of my front against the tile wall. My heart was beating out of my chest as he reached above my fixed palms and pulled two circular things off the hooks on the wall above them. I quickly registered that they were cuffs of some sort, attached by two thick chains that met near the ceiling. There were also numerous handle-looking things placed sporadically along the upper part of the wall as well. I don't know how I missed them before. I was probably too mesmerized by his gorgeous bod, and I guess my peripheral vision had simply registered it as some kind of art.

Wrong!

"Is this okay?" he asked, his voice shaking, hopeful.

I think I managed to squeak out a "Yes," but who the hell knows. I was too fixated on my frazzled nerves. He clapped the padded cuffs around my wrists as a familiar throbbing hammered between my thighs. I was excited and scared and completely turned on. I was learning that fear of the unknown was one hell of an aphrodisiac. What did that say about me?

At that moment, I didn't really care. The fact was, I'd long since made the decision to give myself over to Jesse completely. He hadn't disappointed me yet.

I looked over my shoulder to find him squirting a bottle of clear gel into his hand. "You keep lube in the shower?" I asked.

He snickered. "Not normally. I just hoped we'd end up here at some point tonight. I was dying to try out my newly customized shower stall."

The space was more "watery fuck-box" than shower stall, but okay.

He rubbed the silicone gel around my holiest of holeys, slipping one of his fingers inside to lube up my tight opening. The delightful pressure made me hyper-aware of my pulsating bunghole. He fingered me for a minute before pulling out, causing a shudder to race along my sensitized nerve endings.

He ran his palm along the length of his dick, then positioned it against my ass. "We're gonna take this nice and slow. I want you to tell me everything you're feeling. If you need me to stop at any time, just say so. Okay?"

There was a nervous knot in the pit of my stomach, so all I could manage was a head-nodding, "Okay."

I clamped my eyes closed and flattened my cheek against the wall as I waited for the inevitable pain. I tried to play it cool, but my vibrating body could hardly escape his notice as he pressed the tip of his dick inside. There was pressure, but no undue discomfort, and I started to think that maybe this could happen after all. But Jesse didn't push in any further. It must have been torture for him to hold out, but he kept himself still as he slipped his hands around to my front. One palm grasped my breast and the other went straight for my lady-garden.

"You okay?" he asked, running a finger through my slit.

"Mm hmm. Mmmm..." I moaned unabashedly.

Jesse pinched my nipple as he rubbed my clit. "How 'bout now?"

"*Yesss.*"

I got so caught up in the sensation of his hands that I didn't even realize I'd been pressing my backside against him. With every nudge, his thick cock had been making a leisurely slide further and further inside me. He kept up the motion of his skilled fingers, rubbing my pinkest part, sliding a finger inside my hot cunt. My body strained to accommodate his girth as I felt an overwhelming feeling of fullness, but not all-out pain. Every extra centimeter that his dick entered me was only slightly more uncomfortable than the last. Nothing I couldn't handle. Besides, I was so caught up in the pounding of my throbbing vag that it all managed to feel amazing.

"How we doing?" he asked through sandpaper, his voice hoarse and hungry.

"Good. *So* good," I scratched back.

All I knew was that I wanted to feel him deep inside, fucking me hard. The impulse overwhelmed me. I pressed back with purpose, corkscrewing his dick further into my ass.

Jesse took the cue and thrust his hips forward, burying his pork sword to the hilt. There was a flash of white-hot ache until my body was able to become familiar with the new sensation. The pain quickly subsided once I allowed myself to appreciate how incredible it felt.

He started rocking against me slowly as his hand sped up against my clit. He was the one trembling this time, a realization that almost made me come right then and there. His breathing was hard against my ear—primal, animal sounds that shook me to my core as he pounded into my puckered starfish again and again and again.

"So. Fucking. Tight," he said on a series of thrusts, slamming into my ass, fucking me hard.

I rocked back against him, taking him deep, loving the invasion of his huge cock in my ass and his fingers fucking my cunt. The water rushed over us as my tits smashed against the hard tile with every plunge; my wrists protested in their restraints. *"Fuck me hard, Jesse."*

Jesse impaled me with his dick, balls-deep as he slammed himself inside, grunting on every thrust, swearing against my ear. He pulled his fingers out of me and pinched my nips tightly, sending a shockwave straight to my core.

A chain of obscenities spewed from my mouth, over and over again as my insides throbbed and my bones abandoned me. I could feel my nerve endings gathering at my center, twisting, tightening, until— *"Oh God! Oh fuck! Ohhh!"*—everything detonated outward in an apocalyptic explosion as the universe shattered around me. I screamed and cursed and slumped against the wall, my body supported by nothing more than the restraints at my wrists and Jesse's superhard dick.

He pulled out and spun me around to face him, and I probably looked no better than a slab of meat on a butcher's hook—spent, exhausted, sated.

I got a bit of a second wind as I watched him soaping up his cock, the frothy bubbles gliding across his thick member. God, this man was so beautiful. It really wasn't fair that my body managed to lose all control around him.

"You didn't wait for me," he slithered, a wicked smile decorating his gorgeous face.

"Sorry."

"Don't apologize. Just let me fuck you 'til I come."

I really didn't know how much more I could take. But Jesse stepped closer and slid his hot cock inside its proper hole, and I found I had more energy than I thought. It was impossible to avoid turning into a horny slut whenever that boy came near me. He guided my feet to the strategically placed ledges situated on either side of the stall, gripped the handles on the wall next to my head, and proceeded to thrust that massive member in and out of my body.

Every time he entered me, my back raised against the wall. Every time he pulled out, my slack form sank down onto him. Once he really got going, it caused my body to bounce up and down in a steady rhythm, repetitively impaling me on his cock. I tried to use the ledges at my feet for leverage, but between Jesse's incessant thrusting and my fatigued muscles, I had no control over the situation. I swung like a pendulum from the restraints, and my shoulders felt as if they were ripping from their sockets as my back slammed mercilessly against the hard tile, but I reveled in the pain, feeling everything. His pace picked up as he pounded into me with fevered madness, screwing me with abandon, driving the both of us over the edge. It was like he was trying to fuck all remaining thought out of my head.

Not a far stretch.

I was already exhausted from the first orgasm, but sure enough, my body was gearing up for a second. Just as the stirring started, however, Jesse wrapped an arm tightly around my waist, making animalistic noises against my neck, grunting, swearing, *"Oh fuck, Sugar... I have to... I'm gonna come so fucking hard..."*

At the last second, he pulled out and fisted his dick as jets of hot cum spurted across my skin, decorating my belly like a monochromatic Jackson Pollock painting.

He was as wasted as I was, but he managed to release me from the restraints, the both of us breathless, speechless. My body had gone limp; I was barely able to hold myself upright as I rinsed off. But Jesse had a towel waiting for me, so I slumped into his chest and let him wrap me in his arms. He took such care to pat me dry, kissing every inch of my heated skin as he did so.

My emotions got the best of me in that moment. I don't know if it was simply post-orgasm release or something more, but my eyes started to well up with tears. I felt so completely connected to him. So perfectly matched. So very adored. *Awestruck.*

"Fuck it. You're right." Jesse's comment knocked me out of my musing.

"Right about what?"

"That we're more than just sex." His proclamation startled me, even moreso because his voice was shaking.

"I never said that." *I've thought it, but I never said it.*

"You didn't have to. I can see it every time you look at me. And the thing is, I'm crazy about you right back, Stef. Have been for a long time, in fact."

"You *what?*"

"You heard me."

"I'm not sure I did!"

He stepped closer, wrapping his arms around me again. "You never knew me before. I wasn't always this asshole who had to stick his dick into every woman he met. Even after the breakup with Misty, I didn't go off the deep end. But then I met you, and you were *so* not interested, and I knew I didn't stand a chance. I've been trying to fuck you out of my mind ever since." He dropped his head and shook it, running a hand over his damp hair. "But now... Now that I've had the real thing? There's no going back for me."

His confession was mind-blowing. He'd been "crazy about" me all this time? Through all his snarky comments and all my bitchy retorts... All these months of me being a cold-hearted cuntsicle... and the whole time, he wanted me? "Does that mean...?"

"If you're in, I'm in."

"We don't even like each other."

"Wrong. We're in love with each other."

My eyes went wide at his pronouncement. I knew he meant what he said because Jesse wasn't a liar. In fact, he tended to be *too* honest. And here he was, tossing out the L word. As disbelieving as I wanted to be, the fact was, I knew he was telling me the truth. And—God help me—I was pretty sure I felt the same.

Didn't stop me from messing with him, however. "Two. Hours."

"Huh?"

I raised an eyebrow at him. "It only took you two hours to go from chastising me for talking about our 'relationship' to telling me you're in love with me."

He snickered. "That's what an asshole looks like when he's trying to play it cool. It's a piss-poor defense mechanism; I'm sorry. I just didn't think you could ever be mine."

"What the hell happened in the past two hours that changed your mind about that?"

"I told you. I can see it. Am I wrong?"

I could have played it cool but what would be the point? He was right. He deserved to hear it. I bit my lip, scared to admit it, but forcing myself to do it anyway. "No. You're not wrong." I knew I was fishing, but I didn't care. I wanted to hear him say it again. "Do you really think you're in love with me?"

In true Jesse fashion, he managed to sound sweet and sexy all at the same time as he answered, "Come to my bed. Let me prove it to you. I want to do more than just fuck you tonight."

CHAPTER 10

I let Jesse lead me to his bedroom as a nervous anticipation swirled in my gut. I guess I was expecting a full-on sex dungeon, and I was unsure how whips and chains would factor into our "lovemaking." But instead, I was met with a modest space decorated in gray and black. No handcuffs on the nightstand. No sex swing in the corner. Just a regular old bedroom that would lead anyone to believe Jesse was just a regular old guy.

But I knew better.

The fuzzy thoughts were short-lived, however, once I realized my stomach was still in knots. Yesterday, I was nervous about fucking Jesse, but it was nothing compared to the fear of actually *making love* to him tonight. I took a look at his humongous bed, and anxiously pulled the towel a little tighter across my chest. *Where the enemy sleeps.*

The thing was, after only one short day, Jesse wasn't my enemy anymore. I guess he never was. My mind replayed all the beautiful things he'd said to me—*I'm a one-woman guy. I'm crazy about you. We're in love with each other*—causing a delicious ripple to shiver down my spine. The thought that he had such strong feelings for me was both humbling and gratifying all at once.

He rested a hand on my shoulder as he leaned in to kiss me tenderly, allowing my brain to chill out. His lips were warm and sweet as his fingers slipped into my damp hair and pulled me closer, locking our mouths together. I thought I'd been kissed by this man in every way possible, but here he was, surprising me yet again. His movements were attentive and adoring, patient and reverent.

Time stopped as he peeled off my towel, pulled the comforter from his bed, and lay me down on his cool white sheets, my damp hair splaying across his pillows. He took a moment to appreciate the view, a wicked lip curling as he said, "You are *so* beautiful, Stef."

Not "Sugar." Not "Cupcake." Not any of the nicknames he'd bestowed upon me over the past year. For now, fun and games were over.

The expression on his face was entirely too serious for my comfort as he stripped the towel from his hips and let it drop to the floor. I was struck yet again by the sight of that goddamned body. It was seriously the craziest thing I'd ever seen. I didn't think I'd ever get used to how perfect it was.

He climbed on top of me and brushed a soft kiss across my collarbone, the heat from his mouth in contrast to my chilled skin. He moved his lips over to my shoulder, up to my neck, finally meeting my mouth. He braced his arms on either side of my head as the kiss picked up a bit of steam, and I found myself getting swept away by how sweet it all was. Jesse was a sexy bastard, but here he was, intent on showing me his softer side, and it was almost as erotic as any of our past encounters.

"I'm crazy about you, Stef. Just kissing you is already driving me crazy."

His peen must've been crazy about me too, because I could feel the stiff length of him rubbing against my thigh.

A moan escaped from my throat as I wrapped my arms around him and opened my mouth against his. I pulled him in closer, loving the feel of his bare skin against mine, the weight of him on top of me, of his words, reveling in the tiny bolts of lightning that were shooting through my belly.

His mouth moved down to my neck, licking and tasting and biting as his palm cupped my breast. His lips found their way there, too, and his hot breath caused a shiver to race along my skin as my back arched toward him. He sucked the tip hard, shooting sparks straight to my core, and *holy Jesus I might very well come just from this*.

He worked his mouth down my torso, planting soft licks against my abdomen on his way to my hips, my thighs. Gently, he kissed the spot in between, which almost launched me off the bed. "Oh God, Jesse. I'm already so close."

He chuckled against my pinkest part as his scruffy jaw scratched my inner thighs. Even that felt phenomenal, the abrasiveness heightening every sensation he was stirring within me. He licked me from crack to clit, flattening his tongue and applying more pressure against my wet opening, enthusiastically lapping away and causing me to groan. It was all I could do to keep myself still enough to let him do his thing. My hands fisted in the sheets and I bit my lip as his movements picked up speed. Purpose. Determination.

Jesse switched tactics and started fucking me with his mouth, plunging his tongue in and out of my quivering hole. My head thrashed back and forth on the pillow as the electric charges raced along every nerve ending. And then, without warning, he sucked my clit between his lips and rolled his tongue around the tightened bud.

I saw God.

An inhuman sound roiled from the deepest recesses of my soul as a blinding white flash exploded behind my eyes. I grabbed Jesse's hair in my fist and pulled his face right into my wet cunt, causing him to let out with a heated growl that reverberated throughout my insides. He threw my legs over his shoulders and just went to town on my convulsing vag, his palms gripping my hips as his face buried between my thighs, riding out my climax.

My control already relinquished, Jesse slid his body up the length of mine, slipping his hard cock between my wet thighs, sliding it against my sensitized skin.

He devoured me with his mouth, ramming his tongue deep inside as a distinct humming vibrated in the back of his throat. He pulled back enough to whisper against my lips, "*That was quite a show, Stef. I could go down on you all night.*"

"I'd like to see you try."

"Maybe later. I'm too fucking hard right now I might explode."

We chuckled as I pulled his mouth to mine again, totally making out with his face. He hooked a hand under my leg and hitched it over his hip, grinding himself into me. *Wet-humping. Nice.* I was writhing underneath him, sweaty and slippery and out of my mind, and somehow, the tip of his cock managed to just... slide in.

We both froze in that instant, with the first inch of his cock breaching my entrance and the both of us staring into each other's eyes. I could feel him throbbing against my sensitive rim, his body craving to push in further, but he refused to break.

"Not yet," he scratched out, his voice pure agony. "I didn't want to get here this quick. So many more things I was planning to do to you first."

I could see it was torture for his mind to stay focused on *giving* when all his body wanted to do was *take*. I knew he was trying to prolong our lovemaking, trying to make it good for me, but I was already too far gone. We both looked down to the point at which we were joined, breathing heavily, the both of us trembling with frantic want and desperate need. His resolve wasn't as strong as he liked to think it was, and I got a sadistic thrill from watching as he fell apart.

I knew I was pushing it when I whispered, *"Please, Jesse."*

His entire body trembled at my request as a tense muscle twitched in his jaw. I wiggled ever so slightly, taking him in just a bit more, causing Jesse to grit his teeth and fist a hand against the pillow.

"Stef, I'm dying, here."

I swiped a hand across his jaw and said, "No reason to wait, Jesse."

The inner turmoil played out on his face as his bottom lip quivered, his body tensed in excruciating restraint. Our hearts were beating like mad against one another as the conflict played out in the air between us. We lay like that for an eternity, his cock poised at my entrance, his body coiled, a breath hissing between his teeth... and when he couldn't take it another minute, he pulled out.

I audibly whimpered, moaning from the loss until I realized he was simply reaching inside his nightstand drawer. He quickly rolled on a condom, positioned himself on top of me again, and pushed himself inside. I gasped—a sharp intake of breath that rocked my lungs—from the steel heat sliding inside of me; it was already too much.

He growled against my lips, and I could feel the rumble through my own chest as he pressed his skin to mine. It was so hot to feel so wanted, to know that I was driving this poor guy mad. The muscles of his arms flexed as he caged me with his body, the fruity taste of him invading my senses.

And then he started to move.

Slowly. So slowly I thought I was going to fall apart. He rolled his hips against me, plunging in deep and deliberately, the head of his cock grazing against every ridge along the lining of my sensitive walls. I angled my pelvis to heighten the sensation, and Jesse took the cue, grinding the base of his cock against my clit on every thrust in that same, unhurried rhythm.

The head of his shaft thumped against my G-spot relentlessly as his pubic bone provided the most delicious clitoral stimulation, causing every muscle and nerve ending south of the equator to convulse, my entire body pulsating.

Damn. Who knew slow-fucking could be so hot?

Jesse's brow was sweaty, his face a mask of torment. I could see the anguish there, his fierce determination to do this right, and I didn't know whether to laugh or cry at his predicament.

The thing was, one of the main reasons I fell for this guy was the hot sex. I loved that he was a cad. I loved that he fucked like a beast. I loved everything about him. It was sweet that he wanted to *make love* tonight, but the thing was, he made love to me with everything he said and did. He made love to me with his mouth and his eyes and his beautiful, rocking dick.

Time to let the poor guy off the hook. "You're allowed to fuck me, you know."

The façade cracked.

His eyes darkened with lust as his lip curled into a sneer. The change from Jekyll to Hyde was instantaneous, as if my words had unleashed a monster. *Yeay!*

He growled as he threw my leg over his shoulder and immediately screwed himself in even deeper, stretching my hole to its limits as my body fought to accept his girth. I thought I was going to pass out as he started in with his powerful thrusting, fucking me the way Jesse was meant to fuck. His arms shook as they braced on the bed, already close to losing his control, but still, he kept pounding away at my aching cunt over and over and over again. His head dropped as he cursed, causing beads of sweat to trickle from his hair and drip onto my chest. It was fascinating to watch him fall apart.

His tormented, gravelly voice asked, "You like when I fuck you hard, Sugar?"

Nice to see you again, Jesse Miller. "Yes."

"You like it deep?"

I nodded my head, barely able to find my voice. "*Yes.*"

"I'm gonna come so fucking hard. I'm gonna come on your tits."

My entire body started pulsating again, causing my hands to reach behind me and grab hold of the headboard—not only did I need to brace myself for the impending orgasm tornado, but Jesse liked to overpower me while we fucked—as an involuntary groan escaped from his lips. Primal, animal noises filled the room as he slammed himself inside of me again and again and again, our bodies wet with sweat, tears spilling from my eyes.

The emotional upheaval was overwhelming. I cried out as I came, pulling his ass tighter to me, pulling him in deeper, and Jesse rode the convulsions toward his own climax, fucking me harder and faster, knotting my damp hair in his fists until a guttural boom exploded from his chest as he came, screwing himself into me deep with every pulse of his throbbing dick.

Every muscle in my body was liquefied as he slumped on the bed next to me, the both of us breathing hard, trying to put our world back together.

I looked over at Jesse working the condom off his dick and asked, "What happened to coming on my tits?"

He chuckled, still trying to catch his breath. "Well, I'm still hard. Wanna give me a second chance at the money shot?" he offered playfully before staring down at himself in disbelief. "Jesus. I seriously could go again right now."

"Your dick might be raring to go, but I bet the rest of your body would disagree."

He aimed a deadly smirk in my direction as he teased, "Sugar, I've learned that when it comes to you, nothing is impossible."

* * *

I stirred and squinted an eye at the sun peeking through the curtains. I was barely awake, but I could register the smell of fuck still permeating the room. I opened my eyes to find Jesse, already standing at my bedside, dressed in a pair of boxer briefs and offering a cup of coffee.

"Mornin', Sugar Tits." I gave a stretch before sitting up against the pillows as Jesse asked, "How 'bout some breakfast? You want an omelet?"

Mmm yum. "I may just take you up on that. Do you have stuff to make a Denver? You know—peppers, onions, ham?"

He slid back into bed, conspicuously working a hand under the sheets. "I'm more in the mood for a Greek. You know—feta, spinach, and then I fuck you in the ass."

His comment sent the both of us into a laughing fit. I was legit holding my sides as tears streamed down my face. Jesse pulled me in close and chuckled against my hair.

I caught my breath and snuggled into his arms, inhaling the sleepy warmth of his skin before saying, "Speaking of food and fucking, you know we've still got one helluva mess in that foyer that needs cleaning, right?"

"Shit, you're right," he conceded, swiping a hand over his face. "Tell you what. How about you cook and I'll clean?"

The truth was, I would've much rather stayed in bed and violated him repeatedly.

But alas, a woman cannot live on penis alone.

I took a cleansing breath and resolved to start my day.

Our day.

"Sounds perfect."

EPILOGUE

It's been two weeks since that magical night at Jesse's house.

Since then, we've been inseparable. There's something about the newness of a relationship that turns people into shmoopy dorks. It's like we can't get enough of one another, and yeah, sorry for being all googly-eyed and sappy about it; I know you must find it sickening, but there it is. The fact of the matter is I'm happy and he's happy and goddammit I think we've earned that.

Turns out, I'm good at being in a relationship, at least when it comes to Jesse.

He's not so bad at it himself.

Aside from being a totally hot piece of ass, it turns out that he's also a really great guy. The dude *listens* when I speak, and he's always got some thoughtful advice at the ready. Especially when it comes to work matters. Who knew that a gorgeous body like that could be topped by a fantastic head for business?

I have an interview later this afternoon with a new office manager, and I'm pretty excited about it. I really think she could be The One. My girls have been kicking in with the paperwork the past couple of weeks, freeing me up to do more baking, and Smoochycakes has been thriving ever since. I guess word travels fast in a small town, and once people found out that I was back in the kitchen, business started booming. Things will only improve once I have someone in the office full time.

All the extra income has allowed me to get creative, and I've recently decided to expand our line of Outrageous Cakes. Once I finally have the right manager in place, I'll have the time to officially transform myself into a *baked goods sculptress*.

Jesse's store has always done well, but he's been stepping up his game recently, too. He managed to finagle all our neighboring business owners into participating in a weekend-long party to celebrate the fifth anniversary of The Rimmer Strip Mall.

So, we spent the bulk of yesterday morning blowing up balloons and hanging banners in our windows, readying for the festivities that will kick off in just a few hours later today.

Then we spent most of *last night* fucking each other's brains out.

Some nights we stay at my place, some nights we stay at his, but we always drive into work together, which is a nice way to start my day. I warm up the ovens, he makes the coffee, and then we always find a way to share a few private moments before we're forced to get on with our work day.

Even still, we manage to find the opportunity to grab a few stolen kisses during working hours, indulge in the occasional quickie in one of our stockrooms. I could pretend to be grossed out by such blatant displays of affection but the truth is, I've been loving every minute of it.

I had some last-minute stuff to take care of over at Smoochycakes this morning, so it wasn't until close to six when I was able to meet up with Jesse over at The Market. He was wheeling a metal dolly loaded with crates toward the front of the store, so I bypassed announcing my presence in order to sneak a look at him.

So now, here I am, standing in the doorway like a stalker as I check out his delectable bod. He's wearing his typical kelly-green Market tee and his standard pair of faded jeans. Nothing out of the ordinary, but still, my God... yum.

Without even turning around, he says, "Just got a new shipment of cucumbers, Sugar."

Busted. "Thanks," I laugh out, emerging from my stakeout location and walking toward him, "but I think I'm more into *carrots* these days."

Jesse lets out with a pained groan. "Oh yeah?" he asks, smirking just the slightest bit. "Well maybe you'll find time to give me a little demonstration later..."

He steps away from his busywork to slip his hands around my waist. It's tough to break away, but I only give him a quick peck on his delicious lips before announcing, "I have something to show you first."

Jesse waggles his eyebrows before I lead him through the back door to my kitchen. There on the prep table is the project I've been working on since yesterday afternoon. It's a cake designed as a 3D replica of the fountain out front. It's sitting on a large rectangular base of Gramma Sponge Cake that's been covered in wisps of green frosting. Embedded in the "grass" are dozens of little square cookies, miniature replicas of all the signs from the businesses here in our strip mall.

"Wow, Stef!"

"You like?"

"It's so cool!" Jesse dips his head down to check everything out in greater detail. "Awww and look, you put our cookies next to each other."

His comment is a softball, but I bypass the dirty joke about the proximity of our "cookies."

He raises an eyebrow to snark, "That banana is placed obscenely close to that donut, however."

"That was the idea. We're neighbors, get it?"

"Shit. Is it weird that I've got a semi right now?" he asks, adjusting himself in his jeans.

I roll my eyes and shoot back, "What else is new."

He chuckles as he points to the pile of fondant fruits and veggies. "It's all that phallic produce. It's giving me ideas." I snicker as he steps closer and adds, "Wanna help me out with my eggplant?"

I give a quick glance at the clock, realizing it's almost time to open shop. "We've only got five minutes, Jesse."

"Sugar, if you suck me off properly, I won't need more than two."

I offer him a mischievous smile as my eyes tighten into a sham dirty look. *Lord help me, I'm in love with this kinky bastard.*

I let out with a sigh, grab hold of the bulge in his jeans, and slither, "Drop 'em, Pussy Killer."

THE END

T. Torrest is a pop-culture junkie, a movie aficionado, and a lover of all things 80s.

A lifelong Jersey girl, she currently lives there with her husband and two sons.

Keep turning the pages for a sample chapter of her rock-and-roll romantic comedy,
DOWN THE SHORE!

ACKNOWLEDGMENTS:

I'd like to thank a few people who were either directly or indirectly involved with this book.

First up, my author buddy Heather M. Orgeron for indulging in this ridiculous project with me. You've been supportive of my writing pretty much from the day I first published, and have become an amazing friend over the years (even outside of Book World). I love you so hard, I want to make out with your face. One of these days, we're going to finally wind up in the same room together, and Lord help any innocent bystanders when we do. #shenanigans

To my betas: Thanks for the rushed read! You always have my back. Some of you are cheerleaders, some of you are harsh critics, some of you fall somewhere in between. Every word of feedback from each and every one of you is invaluable. Thank you from the bottom of my ass (it's bigger than my heart).

Thanks to the bloggers! God, I owe my life to you bitches. Thanks for all the enthusiastic pimping.

To my friends and readers: Holy crap. Thank you so much for coming along on this ride. I wrote a book called BANANAS AND DONUTS for fucksake, and look! There you are, reading it! I hope I gave you a giggle or two.

As always, huge thanks and big sloppy kisses to the real-life sugar daddy that lives in my house. Mike, I know the time I spend on my writing is time taken away from our family, and you and the kids have been so understanding in that regard. I love you even more than I love Tastykakes. (That's saying a *lot*.)

Lastly, I'd like to thank God, if only to butter Him up so that He'll keep watch over my children in order to ensure they never stumble upon this book during their lifetimes.

That goes double for my parents.

Praise Jesus!

DOWN THE SHORE

A rock-and-roll romantic comedy.

Livia Chadwick is a photographer by day and a self-proclaimed rock-n-roll junkie by night.

Her dating life is a lackluster parade of evasive jerks and her boss is an unrelenting nightmare of a human being.

What else can a girl do but rent a beach house with her girlfriends and blow off a little steam every weekend?

But hey, she's from Jersey. Barhopping down the shore all season is sort of mandatory.

All is going according to plan… until she meets Jack.

Jack Tanner is a contractor-turned-musician in a small-town cover band suddenly thrust into the limelight.

He's already had enough of the rock-and-roll lifestyle, and groupies have never been his thing.

Then again… there's a gorgeous brunette in the audience tonight, checking him out with the most incredible green eyes he's ever seen.

She's looking for a fling.
He's looking for forever.

It's gonna be one helluva summer.

*Set in the summer of 1995, DOWN THE SHORE
takes the reader on a tour through some of the Jersey
shore's hottest hot spots over one, sleepless, flannel-
clad summer.
It's a look back to a time when the music was
groundbreaking, the rock clubs were king,
and bar bands ruled the world.*

READ WHEN YOU'RE IN THE MOOD FOR:
Sexy, funny, romantic, and nostalgic.

Turn the page for a sample chapter!

Chapter 4

Jack and I have to cross over the crowded dance floor in order to shortcut to the other side of the large club. He's trying to carve out a path for us both when I see him inexplicably reach his hand behind him and blindly grab for mine. I just as inexplicably put my hand in his, and have the oddest feeling as we weave our way through the crowd.

It's kind of... *electric* in a weird sort of way. Our palms are flattened against one another's, our fingers intertwined... It's as though we've performed this act naturally a million times over, not just for the first time one minute ago. The thought has me baffled, but fascinated nonetheless.

Before I know it, he's led me over to the payphones situated near the restrooms. He gives my hand a quick squeeze before releasing his hold and ducking into the men's room.

When Jack lets go, I'm surprised at the loss that washes over me. *What the hell was that?* I don't even know the guy and he has me sweating from simply holding his hand? I can't even imagine what holding his dick will be like. I'll probably pass out.

I spend like an hour digging through the ton of junk in my purse to find the number for the beach house, but it finally appears and I make the call. Even though I'm not in the main part of the club, it's still loud, and I burrow into the alcove as much as I can while covering my free ear with my hand in order to hear.

Samantha answers.

"Hey, Sammy!"

"Hey. Where are you?"

"Tradewinds," I shoot back. "Came to see a band."

"Any good?"

"Yeah, actually. They're fantastic."

I glance up to find Jack leaning against the wall having a cigarette, waiting for me. Fuck. He heard that.

"So, I'm going to assume you'll be spending the night elsewhere?" Sam chuckles at her dig, but it's not like I can take offense. My girls know me too well.

"Well, yeah, but not because... We ran into Monty. We're crashing there tonight."

I thought Jack would've headed back to our friends, but instead, he's just standing there watching me as I talk to Sam. His eyes are squinted as he blows smoke through those delectable lips, practically begging me to suck on them for the next twelve hours or so. Give or take.

"Lucky bitch. Tell him we said hi."

"I will."

Before I can get another word out, I suddenly feel the length of Jack's body pressed against my back. *What the hell?* It catches me by surprise, to say the least.

He chuckles against my hair as he swipes it away and lowers his lips to the back of my neck, my skin shivering at the touch. The whole time, I'm trying to have a human conversation with Sam, no easy feat while this dark prince is ravaging me from behind. I guess he isn't planning on wasting any time before getting this party started, and that is just fine by me. I'm more than game.

I snap back to the real world when I hear Sammy taunt, "Well, have fuuun!"

As if that isn't the understatement of the night. How can a hot rock star against my body be anything but fun? I offer a quick "I'm about to," before giving Sam a rather abrupt goodbye and hanging up, bracing my hand on the wall above the phone to press my backside against him.

At that, he gives out a snicker and whispers against my ear, *"Oh, so you wanna play, do you?"*

Oh, hell yeah I do.

There's an electric current running through my body as he turns me in his arms. He has his hands at my waist, running slowly up and down my sides, and a *just-kidding* smile playing at his lips.

He might be kidding around, but I most certainly am not.

I take a quick look down the hall before backing him against the wall, sliding a hand up his chest and meeting his eyes. I can see the surprise in his, because he has no idea who he's dealing with yet.

"Do I want to play? I thought you'd never ask," I fire back—cheesily, but whatever—watching a sly smile eek across his lips. Lips that I'm about to devour.

I bring my palms around behind his neck, grab a handful of that dark hair in my fist, and pull. He's taken aback by the aggressiveness, but I don't wait for him to figure anything out before rising on my tiptoes and meeting his mouth with mine.

His body stiffens at that, obviously caught off guard, but it doesn't take him long to warm to my advance. Our lips are perfectly matched, our bodies fitting effortlessly against one another's. I feel his muscles relax as he returns my kiss, and soon enough, everything goes insane.

His hands slide around my waist as he pulls me closer against his body, and well, what do we have here? It seems Mr. Happy has decided to join us.

Jack turns us around to slam *my* back against the wall, and holy shit, I think I'm going to die. Our lips meet again and there's a pounding in my ears beyond the blaring music, making me dizzy. His mouth opens, and I can taste his salty, minty flavor, smell the smoky, shaving-cream scent of him, invading my senses, causing me to grip the shirt at his chest and hang on for the ride.

Or maybe I need to take him on one.

I push off the wall and back him through the nearest doorway... which turns out to be a storage closet. But there's a lock on the handle, so I take advantage of that before kissing him again. The smell of bleach and stale beer is permeating my senses as we touch and taste one another, the heat escalating off the charts.

Just as my hand slips down to cop a feel, he asks, "Hey, whoa. Liv. What are you doing?"

The dark is pretty blinding, but I still manage to meet his face, a scowl on mine. "What do you *think* I'm doing?"

He grabs my wrist and places my hand at his waist. Trying to cover for my pounding heart, I slide my palms around to the small of his back, up his spine, across his shoulder blades, and go back in for another kiss. His hair is brushing against my cheek as his tongue invades my mouth, and before I can stop myself, a slight moan escapes from my throat.

I've been with lots of guys before, but something is different with him and I can't quite figure out what it is just yet. He's hot as hell, which is normally my only prerequisite for hooking up with somebody. But this guy has totally upped the ante. He isn't just a rock star. He is a rock GOD. And from the first second I saw him on stage tonight, I knew I was going to wind up here at some point. Well, not here in a freaking closet for godsakes, but here in this guy's naked grasp doing the horizontal happy dance.

Or, I guess, vertical, in this case. TMI?

My hands go back to his jeans, ripping at Jack's fly, but before I can even get the first button undone, he braces his hands at my shoulders and nudges me away. "Whoa, whoa. Take it back some."

Still in a daze, I ask, "What?"

"This isn't happening. Not here."

Since when does a rock star give a shit where I do him? "I locked the damn door. No one's coming in here."

"You got that right. No one's coming *in here*. We can do better than this."

Is he serious? He started this whole thing, and now he's trying to put the brakes on? I'm suddenly struck with the absurd thought that he was only joking around when he attacked me at the pay phones. No freaking way is that possible. Is it?

I cross my arms as my sight adjusts to the dim light, eyeing him up and down. "Is this the part where you try to convince me you're a gentleman? Trying to pretend that you want this to be 'special for me'? Because trust me, Jack, I'm not looking for 'special.' I'm not asking you to work that hard. You can drop the wooing bit."

"*Every* girl is looking for special."

"Not this girl."

He crosses his arms, mocking my pose. "Then what are you looking for?"

"Fun," I shoot back without hesitation. He eyes me in disbelief, so I add, "Do you have a problem with that?"

"Maybe I'm done with fun."

What is WITH this guy? "What's your game, player?"

"No game. Why?"

"You come on like gangbusters, but then the second you find out I'm into it, *bam!* Light switch off."

That makes him chuckle. "Oh, you're a real maneater, aren't you? My mother warned me about girls like you."

"You've never met a girl like me, pal."

"Wanna bet?"

We're staring each other down, and I'm trying not to let him see how humiliated I feel. Here I am, practically throwing myself at his feet, and he's *turning me down.*

Rejection can suck a bag of dicks.

He lowers an eyebrow and sighs, "Look, Liv. I've done this too many times to know that nothing good ever comes out of a situation like this."

"Out of what? A one-night stand? Who says I'm looking for anything more than that to come out of this?"

"Who says I'm *not?*" He lets out an exasperated breath and runs a hand through his hair. "Look. I like you. Can't we just, you know, get to know each other? Do *you* have a problem with *that?*"

Yes. He's messing with my whole M.O. I don't do the 'getting to know you' thing with rock stars. I have mind-blowing sex with them and then go on my merry way. Why is he making this so difficult? "I don't date musicians."

"And I don't fuck groupies."

We stare each other down, caught in a heated standoff. Who the hell does he think he is?

"First of all, I'm not a *groupie.* I'm a music-loving girl with a healthy sexual appetite who knows how to say 'thank you' properly."

"Thank you for what?"

"For being talented as hell, you idiot!"

That brings an unreadable smirk to his lips. I don't have the patience right at the moment to try and explain anything more than that to him, so I continue with my rant. "Secondly, you're not fooling anyone with this chivalry bit. You're a red-blooded male with a working cock that rose to the occasion the second my lips hit yours."

Why the hell is he just standing there smiling at me?

I shake off his smarmy face and line up the kill shot. "Thirdly… Since you don't fuck 'groupies,' feel free to go fuck *yourself.*"

At that, I storm out, leaving him standing there gawking at my retreating form.

Read the rest of Jack and Livia's story anywhere books are sold!